Friendly

Misfortunes

C. L. Conolly

FRIENDLY MISFORTUNES

Copyright © 2014 by C. L. Conolly
Cover and author photo by Julie Witt Photography

C. L. Conolly
clconolly@gmail.com
Cypress, Texas

ISBN-13: 978-0-9886876-1-5

Printed in the United States of America

10 9 8 7 6 5 4 3 2 1

I would like to dedicate this book to
the book club who chose Forbidden Affair and
allowing me to take part in the discussion.
I appreciate each and every one of you for
taking a chance on an unknown author.

Other books by this great author

Forbidden Affair

Friendly

Misfortunes

One

It was senior year in high school. My best friend, Gwendolyn Welsh, and her boyfriend, Sterling Bigum, were waiting for me at our usual lunch table. We had three months left before graduation and five months before we headed off to college.

Gwendolyn was a beautiful girl with thick chocolate brown hair, green eyes and a figure most guys dream about. Sterling was – or at least could have been – an incredibly handsome and charming young man. He had his own style. His blond hair and piercing blue eyes put him right up there on the hottie scale. He could have been popular if he would have dressed better. Shorts that resembled swim trunks with flip flops and a dress shirt with a tie topped off with a tweed jacket was not anyone's idea of cool fashion.

I, on the other hand, had thin stringy hair. I was comfortable in jeans and tee shirts. Once we got to high school, I was glad Gwen continued to be my friend even though I wasn't one of the popular girls. She was pulled into their group and I wasn't allowed to be part of their circle. To the popular girls I was considered fat, so I was left out.

"I got the envelope for UT yesterday. I couldn't bear to open it unless you both got yours too," Gwen said, retrieving a nine by twelve white envelope from her back pack.

"Well, you're in luck. I received mine as well," I said, pulling an identical envelope from my bag.

"I got one too, but it doesn't look like that," Sterling said, producing a standard size number ten envelope.

"That's okay, honey. Let's open them all together," Gwen suggested, kissing Sterling on his cheek.

Gwen and I looked at each other and smiled. Ever since we first met in the third grade and became instant best friends, we had always talked about attending the same university.

She was so shy; when she walked into the classroom she found an empty table and sat alone. I watched her for a few minutes doodle in a notebook before gathering my things together to go over to sit with her. From that moment on we were inseparable.

As we tore open the envelopes, Gwen and I both received an acceptance letter along with a course guidebook. Sterling removed the one page rejection letter and sat moping for the rest of lunch.

"That's okay, sweetie. We can see each other on the weekends and holiday breaks. No worries," Gwen told him.

She turned toward me and we both opened the course guidebook. I looked over everything once then flipped to the courses I needed for law school.

We knew we wouldn't be taking the same classes, but we could request to be roommates in the dorms.

The bell rang to signal lunch was over. We stuffed our college material into our bags and headed for class.

"Hey Gwen, why don't you come over to my house tonight and meet my parents? We can have dinner and talk about our future," Sterling said, just as we arrived to our fourth period. He leaned against the wall and placed his hands on Gwen's hips.

"Sure honey, sounds great," Gwen said, before leaning in for a full on public display of affection. A big no, no in our school.

Our teacher, who was about a hundred years old and wore her glasses around her neck by a chain, poked her head outside the classroom and slapped a metal ruler on the wall just above Sterling's head.

"Don't you have somewhere you need to be young man?" she asked Sterling, when the two love birds jumped apart.

"Yes ma'am, sorry. Bye Gwen, Anjie," Sterling said, nervously as he walked quickly down the hall toward his class.

After school, I drove Gwen to my house to do homework. We settled into my bedroom and pulled our text books and notebooks out of our school bags. Gwen grabbed the phone from my bedside table.

"I should probably call my mother and let her know I am going to Sterling's house for dinner," she said, dialing the number.

Once it started to ring, she pressed the speaker button so I could hear the call. Gwen's mother, Doreen, was a paranoid wack job and I assumed Gwen wanted me to hear the conversation so I couldn't tell her she was overreacting.

"Hello?" Doreen said, when she answered the phone.

"Hey mom," Gwen started. "I'm just calling to let you know I'm going to Sterling's house for dinner tonight. He wants me to meet his parents."

"Are you sure that's a good idea? What do you really know about this boy?" Doreen questioned.

"Mother, you've met him. Several times as a matter of fact and you said he was a nice boy," Gwen said.

"He was a nice boy, but only when he was here. Outside of this house he could be a monster for all I know."

"That's it, you found out his secret. When he comes over he changes into a human boy, but out in the real world he has claws and fangs," Gwen joked.

"That is not what I meant and you know it. Sometimes people appear one way on the outside, but on the inside their brain doesn't differentiate between right and wrong," Doreen lectured.

"I'll be fine Mother. I'm going to dinner at Sterling's house and I'll be home by nine thirty. If I'm going to be any later, I'll call you," Gwen said, before pressing the button to disconnect the call.

"Your mother is a loon," I told her.

"At least you don't have to live with her."

"Oh yeah, your mother makes my mother look like a sane person."

"Thanks Anjenette, so glad the only time you think I'm not crazy is right after you hear the ranting's from Doreen Welsh. Not much of a complement," my mother said, coming in my room carrying a tray of snacks.

"You still come out of the house and watch me walk to my car which is approximately twenty feet from the front door. That's pretty crazy," I told my mother.

"I wish that was all my mother did. She won't let me drive my car unless she is riding with me and she spends the whole time telling me what I'm doing wrong and how that could affect the other drivers around me," Gwen said, shaking her head.

* * *

Around five that day I dropped Gwen off at her boyfriend's house. No one else except Sterling was home when she arrived.

"Do you want me to wait with you?" I asked her, not knowing if he felt like this was going to be his opportunity to make his move on her.

"No, I'll be okay, I promise," she told me.

I watched as she walked up to the front door and rang the bell. He must have been standing right next to the door. As soon as her hand had returned to her side, the door opened and Sterling stood on the other side.

She stepped over the threshold and the door closed behind her. I drove away hoping I was doing the right thing by leaving her alone with him. He just made me feel uneasy sometimes. I felt horrible when she told me about the events that had transpired that evening.

They made their way to the living room and sat down on the sofa. It was normal at first. They watched T.V. waiting for someone to arrive.

"So when do your parents get home?" Gwen asked, once it started getting late.

"It will be later, but if you're hungry I can make you something," Sterling said.

"No, I should probably be getting home. I told my mother I would be home by eight," Gwen lied.

"It is only seven fifteen and you don't live that far from here. You can stay a little while longer," Sterling said, his tone changed to panic.

"I still have some homework that needs to be done." She stood and started for the door.

"NO!" He yelled. "You can't leave me." Sterling grabbed her by her wrists, over powering her and tied her to one of the chairs from the dining room.

When she hadn't made it home by ten, her mother called me. "Have you seen Gwen? She said she was going to Sterling's house after school, but hasn't come home yet. She said she would be back by nine thirty."

"The last time I saw her was when I dropped her off at Sterling's around five. Maybe you should call Sterling," I suggested.

"I tried, but there was no answer at his house. I'm calling the police," she said and hung up.

Two officers went to his house to question Sterling.

"Are you Sterling Bigum?" one officer asked.

"Yes sir," Sterling answered.

"We received a phone call concerning your girlfriend Gwendolyn Welsh. Is she here?"

"No sir. She left a couple of hours ago to go home. She said she still had some homework to do and it was getting late. Did something happen?" He acted concerned.

"She never made it home and her mother seems to believe she is still here," the officer informed.

"Oh no. I knew I should have walked with her. Is there anything I can do to help find her?"

"Just let us know if you see her or think of anything you may have seen that could have been suspicious. A vehicle you've never seen before or someone out walking around that may have looked like they were up to no good."

"No, sir. There was no one around when she left," he told the officer.

"Just let us know if you hear from her."

They had no reason to suspect any fowl play on his part, so they left. He held her captive for three days. As the days turned to night, he would move her to the bedroom and tie her to the bed. He would hold her while they slept and pretend they were a happy couple.

The second night while they lay in his bed, Gwen became curious as to why he was in the master bedroom and his parents hadn't come home yet.

"Where are your parents?" she asked.

"My mother left when I was seven and my father died when I was sixteen," he told her.

"Who do you live with?"

"My aunt and uncle used the insurance money to pay off the house and they allow me to live here alone as long as I go to school, get good grades and stay out of trouble. They visit me once a month to see how I'm doing and stock the house with groceries."

"And you think *this* is staying out of trouble? You can't force me to stay here with you forever, Sterling. Eventually, they will come back here looking for me," Gwendolyn told him.

"By that time you won't want to leave me. You will want to be with me forever. I love you Gwenie and I know you at least care about me," Sterling told her, as he grazed his fingertips across her cheek.

"Please Sterling. Just let me go. This is our senior year. Once we graduate, we can evaluate our relationship and take it from there. This, on the other hand, is not helping the relationship at all."

"I'm sorry Gwendolyn, but I can't let you go. I don't want you to leave me just like both my parents did. I don't like being alone," he pleaded with her.

"So ask your aunt and uncle to stay with you. Please Sterling, just let me go," she begged.

"Shhh, it has been a long day and you need to get some sleep."

At the end of the third day, while he was in the process of transferring her from the chair to the bed, the doorbell rang. Sterling quickly took her to the bedroom, tied her up to the bed, then walked down the stairs to answer the door.

Two detectives stood on the other side of the threshold with a search warrant and six uniformed officers.

"Sterling Bigum, we have a warrant to search the premises," one detective said before storming through the door with the officers at his heels.

The other detective led Sterling into the dining room. He told him to have a seat.

"I'm detective McKinney. I'm just going to sit here with you until they finish searching the house. Can I get you anything?"

"This is my house. If I want anything, I'll get it myself," Sterling said defiantly.

"You're not getting up from that chair until the search is complete."

"We found her!" A shout came from upstairs.

"Sterling Bigum, you're under arrest for kidnapping. Please stand up and place your hands flat on the table." McKinney arrested Sterling and the officers brought Gwendolyn downstairs.

As she was being escorted through the front door, she turned and made eye contact with her captor. She was ushered out to an awaiting ambulance.

Sterling was charged and pled guilty to kidnapping. He was sentenced to ten years imprisonment.

After high school Gwen and I both went on to the University of Texas, until I was accepted into law school. She graduated with a degree in journalism and moved back with her parents. I moved on to law school and made sure to keep in touch. Whenever I was available, Gwen and I made plans to see each other.

Gwen's mother was overbearing and paranoid, so she was ready to get out of her parent's house. She was unable to live on her own being paid a freelancer income. Once I graduated, we decided to move in together.

Being a model prisoner, Sterling was paroled after five years and ever since, Gwen has been afraid to leave the house alone. She was turning into an agoraphobic hermit and I was determined to help her live a normal life. Every Sunday the two of us went to her parents' house for lunch, then headed over to my parents' house for dinner. I had promised her family I would keep her safe. That was one promise I planned to keep.

TWO

I was relieved and frustrated to be leaving the court house early on a Friday afternoon. I was prosecuting a case where a woman was accusing her landlord of installing video equipment throughout her apartment. He claimed it was surveillance video only to capture thieves if someone were to break in. Luckily, the law was on my side since one of those cameras just so happened to be pointed directly into her shower.

I was able to obtain the warrant for the videos when conveniently they had disappeared. The defense argued that without the tapes my client couldn't prove she was being recorded while bathing. I had photographs of the cameras where they were installed in the apartment as well as a video I had recorded explaining what each camera was capturing. Unfortunately, that wasn't good enough and the judge recessed court until Monday and told the defense attorney that the tapes better reappear by then.

I stood on the steps out front and looked at the sky. It was a beautiful afternoon to drive a convertible with the top down. Regrettably, I drove a sport utility vehicle. My first stop was the law office I worked at to drop off the court papers from the case. It had been a long week and I couldn't wait to get home.

As I drove down the street toward the twenty five story office structure, I was praying the building was empty. I was ready for the weekend to begin and knew if anyone was in the office I would be sucked into working over the weekend. My boss was all about the money. He couldn't care less about the client. If I had time over the weekend to dig up more evidence on the defendant in order to end the trial quicker so he could have his money and we could move on to the next case, he would find a way to guilt me into staying.

I pulled into the parking garage and was relieved to see only a few cars. I was hoping that meant I wouldn't be delayed getting home. I took note of each vehicle as I walked toward the elevator. I didn't see my boss's Mercedes, which I felt was a wonderful thing.

I rode the elevator up to the twenty second floor and walked as fast as I could to my office. Luckily, I didn't see anyone there, so I was able to drop off the files and ride the elevator back down to the garage without being stopped.

As I approached my SUV, I noticed Mateo Cray, a scumbag pervert I had prosecuted for a client who had claimed he raped her, leaning against the back hatch. The judge ruled in favor of my client and ordered him to pay all her legal fees. I was the one who had the privilege of contacting him every two weeks for payment.

He stood and straightened his clothing as soon as he saw me approaching. All I could think was 'Great, which part of my body is he going to longingly stare at today?'

Mateo dressed like an English professor. He wore blue jeans with a button down dress shirt, a tie and a brown tweed jacket. He was always making references to me about us going out, but he gave off a creepy psycho vibe and made my skin crawl. He took sexual harassment to another level. Whenever we had to meet, so I could pick up his payment, he was always eye balling all the secretaries and paralegals in the office. I was sure that if every one of the women he had ever come in contact with were standing behind a pass through window and all he could see were our faces, he would have no idea who we were.

When he first started coming to the office, I wanted to be nice. It was in my nature to make sure everyone felt comfortable in the law office because the older lawyers were harsh and most of our female clients were uncomfortable talking to them. I knew that was the reason he had latched on to me.

If I had known he was going to become infatuated with me, I would have treated him the way the other lawyers did. Over the past few months, his obsession had become almost violent.

One night I was working late and everyone else had gone home. I had no idea Mateo was lurking in the building. I left my office to go to the kitchen for a cup of coffee when he approached me in the hallway.

"Hey there, working late?" he said, staring at my chest.

"Hello Mateo. Yes I am. What are you doing here? We aren't scheduled to meet for another couple of days. You need to leave," I told him, trying to get past him to the kitchen.

"Do you need any help?"

"No thank you. You can go home."

"I don't think it is safe for you to be here alone," Mateo said, stepping closer to me until my back was pressed against the wall.

"I'll be fine, just go," I said, as I again tried to get past him.

He punched the wall next to my head, then pointed his stubby finger at my face. He was almost touching my nose.

"You better watch out," he said, before grazing my cheek with his fingertips, taking one last look at my breasts then walking away.

That memory haunted me every time I had to meet him in the office and this time was no exception. I was pretty good about putting up a tough girl front when all I really wanted to do was curl up in a corner in the fetal position and cry.

"Mateo, to what do I owe the pleasure?" I said, with slight sarcasm as I stepped up next to my vehicle.

"A pretty little thing like you shouldn't be walking alone, at night, in a dark parking garage. Let me escort you." He wiggled his caterpillar like eyebrows at me as if he were expecting me to swoon.

"First of all, it is only late afternoon, not night. There are lights on everywhere here in the garage anyway and it is still daylight. Plus, Hank the security guard is in his booth over there." I waved at Hank.

"Anjenette, please. What would Hank do if someone were to run up to you with a gun and try to abduct you? He's almost ninety years old."

"I own a Taser, you know that," I said, referring to the time he was harassing one of the secretaries and I had no other option, but to bring him to his knees. "I can protect myself. I also take self-defense classes and kickboxing. Technically, I could kick your ass."

"Abductions can happen at any time of day. If a woman is walking alone she is the prime target for an abduction and possible rape," he said, in a sultry tone as if he was trying to turn me on.

"Okay Mateo, I'll take your advice with a grain of salt. Thank you," I told him, sarcastically.

I pressed the button on my key fob and disengaged the alarm. Reaching for the driver's side door to let myself in, Mateo pressed his hand up against the door preventing me from opening it.

"You really should be a little more careful considering the fact that you prosecute a lot of scumbags. Someone could want you dead," he warned.

"And maybe you should find someone else to harass," I retorted, knocking his arm away.

Opening the door, I lowered myself into the driver's seat and locked the doors immediately. I shifted the car into reverse as soon as the engine turned over.

He stepped over to the row of cars in the parking spaces behind me as I backed out of the parking space and shifted the car into drive. Before I was able to transfer my foot from the break to the gas pedal, I heard Mateo shout, "You better watch your back bitch."

I rolled my driver's side window down and leaned out, "Really Mateo? What are you going to do?"

He reached into the waistband of his pants and produced a hand gun. He raised it into the air and shot out one of the overhead lights above my car. Glass rained down around my vehicle.

"Mateo, what the hell?" I yelled.

I saw Hank stand and emerge from his booth. I wasn't sure what he could do other than call the police.

"The next one is for you," he said, aiming the gun at me.

I rolled up the window and took off. As I drove past Hank, I saw he was on the phone, hopefully calling the police.

With my heart racing and my hands trembling, I sped all the way home.

Three

I pulled up into the driveway of the dwelling I shared with Gwendolyn. My heart beat had slowed and I could no longer feel it as if it were trying to escape from my chest. Once I crossed the threshold into the house, I saw Gwen lounging on the sofa in the living room, with a book. I could tell she was attempting to pretend she wasn't waiting for me.

"Oh, you're home. Good, I have something to tell you," Gwen said.

"What's going on?" I asked, not showing any fear. I didn't want her to know anything had happened.

"Well Anjenette, I have booked us a three day and two night mini-vacation at the best resort in town. It is for the three day Memorial weekend you get in a couple weeks. There's a spa and a pool and private massages," she said, excited.

"Are you sure this is something you're ready for?" I asked. "At some point we could get separated."

"Separated, what do you mean by that?"

"I'm just saying. It could happen."

"Why would it happen? This is supposed to be a weekend for the two of us to spend together. We should never be apart." The fear in her voice was apparent.

"You never leave the house alone. Someone always has to be with you and when we are out in public, you are so paranoid we are only out for a couple hours before you freak out and we have to come home. How are we going to eat?" I inquired.

"Room service. If we go to the café in the lobby, I would be alone if either of us has to go to the bathroom," she responded.

"How would that be any different than us sitting at home and ordering takeout?"

"I need to get out of this house and stop being so scared of my own shadow. You need a little relaxation and a massage could do you a lot of good. Please Anjie? We could both use this." She folded her hands together and rested her chin on her interlaced fingers as if she was begging.

"Fine, Gwen. We really could use a mini-vacay. Get all the information together and we will present it to our parents on Sunday."

She jumped up off the couch, slammed her body into mine and wrapped her arms around me. She squeezed me so tight I could feel the excitement she radiated.

"I was able to get this package for two. It's nothing weird. It's for a girl's weekend. I have been planning this for over a month. I can make up a schedule for us and even vlog about it. Maybe if I include them in my vlog they could give us a free weekend or something. Wouldn't that be exciting?"

She ran off up the stairs and I went into the kitchen to start dinner.

Saturday afternoon, while I was doing laundry, Gwendolyn came running down the stairs almost tripping over her own feet. I heard her feet stop in the dining room.

"Anjenette!" She yelled over the sound of the washer and dryer.

I threw down the towel I was folding and ran out into the dining room. My heart was racing. The urgency in her voice sounded as though she was hurt. "What happened?" I asked, as I slid to a stop, my eyes wide with panic.

"I have the entire package for our weekend set up and I want you to take a look at it," she said, pushing a green colored file folder across the table toward me.

I shifted my gaze from the folder to her, then back to the folder again. "Have you lost your mind? Why did you scream like that?" I asked, placing my hand on my chest and looking up at her again. My heart felt as though it was trying to bust out.

"I wanted to make sure you could hear me," she said, leaning across the table and tapping her finger on the file. She was trying to divert my attention back to what she wanted to show me.

I opened the folder and saw a beautifully put together presentation. I pulled back the clear cover and skimmed over the pages. There was a schedule for each day of our entire weekend. She had also added photos of the resort and photo shopped us into some of the pictures to show us relaxing by the pool and enjoying a massage.

"You have really put a lot of thought into this. Every minute of every day is planned out. This is perfect. I think your parents will be very pleased and excited to let you go," I told her.

"You really think so?" she asked.

"I know how over protective your parents have been since the incident with Sterling. I think they will be willing to even help pay for it," I laughed.

"You don't think my mother will completely disregard the whole idea saying it is silly and dangerous like she does every time we talk about going shopping?" she asked, seemingly afraid of the answer.

"Gwen, you have put together an entire package that no one can say no to. I had reservations at first too, but now I am thinking this is a great idea."

"I know, right? They can't reject this vacation. We both need this," she commented, pulling the folder back across the table toward her.

She skipped over and placed the file on the table by the front door so we wouldn't forget it for the next day. Gwen was in such a good mood for the rest of the day, she decided to help me with the chores.

Sunday morning I woke up to the smell of breakfast. I was surprised considering Gwen had never used the stove or oven since I had known her because her mother had warned her about the dangers of fire and gas poisoning.

I descended the stairs slowly, half expecting to see my mother in the kitchen cooking. When I realized Gwen was the only one there admiring the array of food on the table, I joined her in the dining area.

"What is this?" I asked.

"I made breakfast for us," she said, pointing out the eggs, pancakes and toast.

"You actually used the stove?"

"Well, I've seen you use it tons of times without anything bad happening; so I figured what's the harm. Now, sit down and I'll get the condiments and juice."

We enjoyed a wonderful breakfast and a relaxing morning. She had done a really great job for it being her first time ever cooking anything.

That afternoon we were heading out to Gwendolyn's parents' house, when out of nowhere, she decided she didn't want to go. She was crying and hyperventilating.

"Gwenie, what's wrong?" I asked.

"I can't do this. I can't handle my mother's condescending tone and rejection," she said, before running up the stairs.

The door to her bedroom slammed shut and I was left standing in the open doorway dumbfounded.

I set her vacation proposal down on the table, closed – and locked – the front door, then headed upstairs to find out what was wrong with her.

"Gwendolyn Marie Welsh, why are you acting like this right now? We need to go," I said, in a mommy voice to the closed door.

"I'm not going. My parents are never going to approve it. I don't want the disappointment."

I could tell by her voice she was crying. "Gwenie, come on. You did a wonderful job on the presentation; how can they say no?"

"I was held hostage, Anjenette."

"That was eight years ago, Gwen. They can't hold you back forever and keep you from experiencing things." I turned the knob and opened the door. "Come on, get up," I encouraged.

"I can't go. This was a bad idea. Tell them I'm sick or something," she said, with her face buried into her pillow."

"Look," I said, sitting down on the bed. "You can do this. Don't get discouraged. I'll help you if you need it. Come on, get up."

"No, my mother says the real world is filled with dangerous monsters that are always out there, waiting for some unsuspecting sweet girl to steal from her family. She says they have sick desires and they can only fulfill that desire by taking from others," she said.

"That is your mother's way to make sure you stay dependent on her instead of experiencing life on your own like everyone else in the world." I stood up and looked down at her with my hands on my hips. "This is your time Gwen. Your time to experience the world the way God intended. You only live once and what way is it to live if you live in fear? You need some fun in your life and I'm going to help you have fun. Now, get out of bed and let's go show your mother that you have decided to take over your own life."

She lifted her head up and looked at me. "You think she'll be okay with that?"

"Absolutely not, but it's worth a try. Now let's go, but you might want to run a brush through your hair first."

We both laughed and she scurried off into the bathroom.

By the time we made it to her parents' house we were twenty minutes late. Gwen's mother came running out the front door towards the car.

"Where have you been? I almost called the police!" Gwendolyn's mother yelled through the open passenger door at me.

"We are only a little late, Doreen. I'm sorry," I apologized.

"Well, you're here now. Come on inside for lunch." She stepped back and allowed Gwen to get out of the car. "Are you okay? You're not hurt, are you?"

"No mom, I'm fine. You can't hold me back from experiencing life forever," Gwen said, as she walked past her mother into the house.

"That sounds like something you would say," Doreen said, in an accusatory tone; mostly *at* me, rather than *to* me.

I was left sitting in my car as Gwen and Doreen headed inside. I knew the only reason Doreen treated me the way she did was because I had convinced Gwen to move in with me instead of staying at her parent's house forever. At least her father was on my side.

I exited the vehicle and closed the door. The last one to enter the house and I was thinking 'Thank goodness Doreen didn't lock me out'.

Gwen's parents were antique collectors. Every inch of their house proved that, from the sofas and the cabinets to the stove and most of the appliances. It looked like the twenties and thirties threw up.

I found Gwen and her father in the family room and joined them.

"So Laird, how is everything here on the home front?" I asked him.

"Doreen is always worried about Gwen. If they aren't talking on the phone, Doreen is talking about Gwen. Are you taking good care of our little girl Anjie?"

"Of course sir. Nothing but the best, for the best." I leaned down and hugged him.

"Come on the three of you. Lunch is on the table," Doreen shouted from the dining room.

Four

After lunch, Laird returned to the family room to continue doing whatever he was in the process of before we arrived. Doreen, Gwen and I had cleared the table and cleaned the kitchen. Once we had finished, we joined Laird for Gwen's vacation proposal.

Laird sat in his chair while Gwen and I sat across from him on the sofa and Doreen took her seat on the love seat. Gwen pulled out her vacation proposal and began her presentation.

"Mom, Dad, I know we have been through a lot. Most of it has happened to me. I need a vacation." Gwen handed each of her parents a proposal package she had prepared.

"What is this?" Doreen asked.

"Please hold all questions until the end. As you know, there is a three day weekend coming up. I have planned a spa weekend for Anjenette and me. We will be staying at the Rizzy Hotel and Spa in Sundaisy. There, they have Hot Rocks Beauty Spa with specialty trained staff for optimum relaxation. We will be staying three days and two nights. It is only a few hours from here so we won't be far.

"We arrive Friday any time after five for check-in. Saturday we have breakfast at eight, a full body massage at ten, lunch at eleven thirty. Then we have a facial and mud bath at one and a mani/pedi at two. Around four we are to have a relaxing walk before dinner in the hotel restaurant at five thirty.

"After we have finished with dinner, it is just us time. The two of us can do whatever we want until we go to bed." Gwen smiled with a look of satisfaction on her face.

"That sounds nice, but what about Sterling? He's not locked up anymore," Doreen said, with concern.

"We haven't seen him in years. He has probably moved on with his life and forgotten all about me. Come on, mom. I'm a grown up now and would like to live like one. I am tired of living in fear of something that may never happen."

"This is your fault," Doreen directed at me. "If you would have just left her here with us rather than insisting she go live with you, she would be happy to stay home."

She always knew how to talk to me to make me feel like insignificant shit. A part of me wanted to apologize to her that I made her feel that way and the other part wanted to tell her to go to hell. I went with the latter.

"If she stayed with you, she would be an agoraphobic child who would never experience anything a normal adult should. Don't blame me for her having a mind of her own," I spat at Gwen's mother.

"How dare you? How dare you speak to me that way? You should show me more respect," Doreen said.

"Come on Gwen. We have vacation plans to make. Let's go." My eyes were fixed on Doreen as I helped Gwen to her feet so we could leave.

"Hold it. You're not taking her anywhere. She is going to stay here with us," Doreen informed, grabbing Gwen's other arm.

"First of all, let me go," Gwen began, as she yanked her arms away from both of us. "Second, I don't appreciate the two of you talking about me like I'm not here. Mom, I can make my own decisions and this vacation was my idea. I didn't even want to come today because this is how I thought you would react.

"Anjenette, I appreciate your enthusiasm, but I need to fight my own battles. Mom, we are going and that is that. Let's go Anjie." Gwen grabbed my wrist and ushered me toward the door.

"Love you Dad," Gwen said, before closing the front door behind her.

By the time we had made it out to the car, Gwen was breathing so heavily I thought she was going to have another panic attack. "Gwenie, you need to slow down your breathing before you hyperventilate and pass out," I told her, as she leaned against the passenger door.

"I can't believe I spoke to my mother like that. What was I thinking? It was so disrespectful."

"Be proud of the way you handled yourself. She needed to hear that. You are your own person," I encouraged.

"I guess. I hope she's not mad at me."

"You need to live your own life and hope that someday she realizes you are an adult. Get in, let's go see my parents," I told her, as I walked around to the driver's side of my car.

When we pulled up to my parents' house we ended up being an hour early. My mother was sitting on the porch swing and waived without getting up.

"How're y'all doing?" she shouted, as we exited the vehicle.

"We had an eventful afternoon," I told her, as I approached.

"Well, have a seat and tell me all about it. Gwendolyn, are you okay?"

She had a faraway look on her face and her eyes were glazed over. "I can't believe I talked to my mother like that," was all Gwen could say.

"What happened?" my mother asked.

"Well, let's go inside first. We have something we would like to present to you and Dad," I said.

The three of us headed into the house. My father was lounging on the chaise in their reading room reading one of his favorite classics by Ernest Hemmingway. He was so enthralled he never even noticed we had entered the room. I walked over and gave him a kiss on the cheek. Snapping out of his reading coma, looking up and seeming disoriented, it was almost as though he had just been awakened.

"Oh, hello darlings," my father said, to both Gwendolyn and me.

"Dad, Gwen and I have something we would like to discuss with you and Mom. Do you have a moment?" I asked him.

"Of course. Come on girls, have a seat." He motioned toward the sofa.

Gwen went ahead and presented the vacation to my parents. She sounded nervous and spoke in such a way that she had almost expected them to react the same way her parents did. When she was finished, I could see the shock on her face by their reactions. They were impressed by her research and planning.

"Nicely done," my mother said, as she stood up and applauded.

"Good job Gwenie. Maybe you should be a travel agent," my father told her.

"I might actually look into that when we get back," Gwen said, smiling. She sat up straight and genuinely looked happy and satisfied with herself.

"You really should. You presented that vacation so well, even I want to go," he said, reaching out to grab Gwen's hand.

"So, can you tell me now how your morning was eventful?" my mother asked, with her hands pressed together and the tips of her fingers drumming against each other.

It was almost as if she knew we were going to speak ill of Doreen. My mother loved it when we complained about Gwen's mother. Her expression always showed her craving for it.

I began the story with irritation and anger, explaining Gwen's parents' facial expressions and body language. Gwen ended it in tears as she described their reaction and how I acted and what she had said to her mother.

"I can't believe I talked to my mother like that," she said afterward, tears streaming down her face.

My dad stood up for the first time since we had arrived and hugged Gwendolyn. She wrapped her arms around him and really started to cry.

"We are so proud of you. The way you handled yourself, shows maturity. You two go on that vacation and have fun," my dad said, then kissed Gwen on her cheek.

Five

Once my parents were able to meet her, they had always encouraged Gwen to be her own person and managed to make her feel better after her mother would tear down her self-esteem. Doreen has always discouraged her from trusting others and would prefer her to be a hermit in order to shield her from the bad people in the world. Doreen tried to home school Gwen for a couple of years.

"Honey, don't you think this is holding her back developmentally since she has never had any interaction with other children her own age?" Laird asked Doreen, when Gwen was six and still being taught a curriculum for kindergarten.

"She is safe here. Someone could hurt her out there. Do you have any idea how many bad people there are in the world? She could be kidnapped or worse a neighbor could molest her. I am not taking the chance by letting her out of this house," Doreen told him.

"She needs to go to an actual school and you need to let go. When we were growing up, all of the same dangers existed. The only difference is the fact that now it is publicized. Back in our day no one ever wanted to talk about what happened to little Tommy and why his parents moved away. No one ever talked about why Suzie always looked scared when she emerged from the Smith house. Everything was cotton candy and lolly pops until the media started talking. You need to let her go out there and be a kid, not terrify her with your cockamamie stories about what could happen."

By second grade she was in public school and Doreen felt the area they were living in wasn't safe for her little girl. They found a better school district and moved.

Two weeks after Gwen and I had met, I asked her if she would like to stay over at my house for the weekend.

"I'll ask my mom. She's kind of weird about me staying anywhere without her," Gwen said.

I was so excited. I went home and had my mother help me set up a camp out in the living room. I waited for hours for her to call and say she was coming over, but the call never came. I called her house a couple of times over that weekend, but no one ever answered the phone. By Monday morning I was so sad I didn't even want to go to school.

"You should go and find out what happened. Maybe she had a family emergency and had to leave suddenly," my mother told me.

When I saw Gwen in class she wouldn't talk to me or sit at the table with me. It was a whole week before I could get her to even look at me.

"What happened?" I asked when I was finally able to get her to talk to me.

"My mother said you were going to use me as a sacrifice in a cult ritual. I was scared to listen to anything you had to say. She said you were going to try to brain wash me into believing my parents were evil."

"Why would I do that? You're my friend. And what is a cult?"

"I don't know, but she seems to think everyone is a member of one," Gwen said shrugging.

"Your mom is weird," I told her.

"Yeah, I talked to my dad and he told me not to take anything she says too literally because most of what she says is just crazy ranting. I'm not able to stay at your house, but my mother says if you would like to come over to my house for a supervised visit she would be willing to consider it," Gwen said, smiling.

Even at eight years old I knew I was going to have to convince Gwen somehow that her mother was too overprotective.

It wasn't until middle school that Gwen was able to realize I really was her friend and her mother was just crazy. We were in seventh grade and I was only allowed to see Gwen outside of school if we were at her house and her mother was right there the whole time. If we went outside to play, Doreen would sit in her lawn chair on the driveway and watch us. We weren't ever allowed to play hide and seek. If Doreen couldn't see her precious daughter, it wasn't a safe game.

At thirteen I was able to convince my mother to call Doreen so they could meet and she could prove she wasn't a member of a cult that sacrificed children. The three of us were invited to the Welsh house for dinner. Of course it was a premade meal she had ordered. Doreen's irrational fear of the oven and stove causing the house to engulf in flames was one more thing to check off on the nut house enrollment form.

"I'm so glad we are able to do this. The girls have been friends for such a long time, it is about time we got to meet," my mother told Doreen when we arrived.

Doreen just flashed a fake smile and pretended to agree. Laird took my father into the living room and they sat down on the couch to watch football. Gwen and I started down the hall toward her bedroom.

"Where do you two think you are going?" Doreen asked just before we were out of sight.

"We were just going to go to my room and do each other's hair for dinner," Gwen said.

"I don't think so young lady. Do you know how many young girls are taken from their families when someone sneaks into their bedroom window when they are in there just fixing their hair?" her mother started.

"Too many," Gwen said, irritated.

"That's right, too many. You two are going to stay where I can see you at all times. Anjenette, you know that is the rule in my house," she scolded.

"Yes ma'am," I answered.

"Thank you. Now, why don't the two of you hang out with your fathers in the living room until dinner is ready?"

My mother just stood there with a dumbfounded look on her face as she listened to Doreen spill nonsense out of her mouth. She waited until they were in the kitchen before confronting Doreen.

"You don't really believe that crap you're saying do you?" my mother started.

"Excuse me? My child is the most important person in the world to me. I'm sorry you don't feel the same way about yours," Doreen accused my mother.

"You are out of line here lady. I do everything in my power to protect my little girl. You have to let them go out there and experience the world for themselves," my mother said, rage in her voice.

"She can experience the world when she is an adult and able to protect herself. Until then, I am going to keep an eye on her and protect her for as long as I can."

"The only thing you are doing is hurting her, not protecting her. When she finally does grow up, which in case you haven't noticed is happening right before your eyes, she is going to be so scared of the world she will probably never leave your house. She will never meet new people, she will never get married and she will never have any kids. All of the greatest joys in life you will have robbed from her because you have depicted the world as a scary place to be. She will probably live with you forever and wait for the sweet release of death when she can be free of all the evil in the world," my mother was screaming at her.

"Get out of my house! You are no longer welcome here! Get your demon spawn and leave my house! Gwendolyn, you are no longer allowed to speak to that girl!" Doreen's voice was a high pitched shrill.

"Now wait just a minute here," my father piped up. He and Laird had gone to the kitchen when they heard the yelling. "My daughter is not a demon and I don't appreciate you insinuating so. I think you need to calm down and we should sit down and have a rational discussion like adults, rather than accusing each other of who is ruining whose daughter's life."

"Did you not just hear what your wife said to me?" Doreen complained.

"Oh I heard every word. I think the neighbors heard every word, from both of you. We are going to send the girls into Gwen's bedroom and we are going to have a grown up discussion," my father said, as Laird went back to the living room and shut off the television, then ushered Gwen and I to her bedroom.

"Close the door and turn on your radio. You girls don't need to hear what we are going to talk about," Laird told us, before returning to the living room.

"Oh I'll close the door, but I'm not going to turn on the radio. I want to know what is going on. I am so tired of being stuck in this house. You go outside all the time alone and you're still here," Gwen said, once her father left down the hallway. She pressed her ear against the door.

"Did something happen recently? Your mother seems extra crazy today," I asked, sitting on the edge of the bed.

"The news reported about a fourteen year old girl who was abducted from her home, raped repeatedly then murdered. She is still reeling from the story."

Our parents were able to talk quietly enough we didn't hear anything. After about an hour, we were called out to have dinner.

"Gwendolyn, your mother has something she would like say," Laird told his daughter.

"Sweetie, these people want to take you to their house. I don't think it is a good idea, but your father seems to think it will help your social skills. If at any time you want to come home, just call me and I will come get you," Doreen told her.

"Do you really mean it momma? I can go?" Gwen clarified.

"Yes, you can go," Doreen said, tears forming in her eyes.

"Can we set up your living room the way you did when we were eight?" Gwen asked me.

"Absolutely. Let's go get some of your stuff," I said, grabbing her by the arm and pulling her toward her room.

It was that night, when we were alone camping in my living room that Gwen realized her mother's fear and exaggeration was unfoundedly superficial. The only thing that happened to us that night was fun.

Six

I was able to get out of work early on the Friday to begin my three day weekend mini vacation with Gwen at one o' clock. It only took us two hours to arrive at the hotel. The whole way there Gwen talked about how much fun we were going to have. We arrived at the hotel too early for check in, so we left our luggage in the car and went in to explore the where we would be staying.

The hotel was thirteen floors, only twelve of which had rooms. The first floor was all recreational. The lobby was right inside the automatic double doors. To the left was a hallway that went around the back to an area where the indoor pool was located along with a bar and a billiards area with four pool tables. Just past the bar was the restaurant.

To the right of the lobby were six conference rooms and at the end of that hallway was the spa we were there to enjoy.

"I know check in is at five, but let's see if we can check in early and go swimming," Gwen said.

We headed up to the front desk where a very colorful young man of about nineteen stood. His nametag read Spencer.

"Good afternoon ladies. How may I help you?" he asked.

"We have a reservation under Marcum-Welsh. I was told our check in time would be five, but I was hoping we could check in early since we are here," Gwen told him.

"Well, let's check the status of your room," he said, as he began tapping away at the keys on his keyboard. "You're in luck. They have just finished cleaning the room and it is ready for check in."

He tapped a few more keys, pulled out two key cards from the drawer next to him and swiped them at the computer. "Okay, you are in room four oh two. Here you go." He handed us the cards.

"Thank you, Spencer," Gwen said, as we walked back out to the parking lot to grab our luggage.

We went up to the room, unlocked the door and stepped inside. It was equipped with two double beds, a small love seat and a round table near the sliding glass doors that opened to a balcony to look out over the small town.

We placed our bags on our beds, changed into our swimsuits and headed down to the pool. It was nice having an indoor pool. The plus side, we didn't have to wear sunscreen. The down side was no sun for tanning. Luckily, the hotel did have a sun deck for that purpose with lounge chairs and umbrellas, along with servers bringing us drinks.

We spent half an hour on the sun deck and half an hour cooling off in the pool before heading back up to the room to shower and change.

"What did you want to do first?" I asked Gwen.

"Since we are early, how about we get something to eat? I'm starving," she said, rubbing her belly.

"Let's forget room service, we could order food to be delivered at home. Do you want to go to the café downstairs in the lobby or somewhere out?"

"My plan was not to leave the hotel the entire weekend. Let's just go to the lobby." Gwen smiled.

She acted like a teenage girl whose parents allowed her to go on a trip unsupervised. She grabbed my hand and headed for the door.

"This is going to be the best weekend of my life," Gwen said as we waited for the elevator.

"With more to come," I told her.

The hotel café was small and simple. The hosts stand at the entrance, a few booths to the right, some tables to the left, a buffet line and the kitchen in the middle. The buffet was only open for breakfast so the hostess sat us with menus.

We discussed our schedule for the weekend. We had dinner, went back up to the room and watched television until we fell asleep.

The next morning we headed back down to the café for breakfast. From the time we got up to the time we took our first sip of coffee, we were silent.

"We have enough time to enjoy our coffee and eggs before heading on to our massages. We both really need to relax. Hopefully this weekend will help," Gwen said, taking another swig of coffee.

"If it helps enough, maybe we should send your parents on one of these relaxing weekends," I said.

Gwen laughed with such gusto. I thought coffee was going to spray from her nose.

"That would be great to see the look on my mother's face when presented with two tickets to a spa weekend. We could tell her it is to help remove the stick out of her ass. She will be so relaxed it might just slide right out."

That time, *I* laughed so hard I thought coffee would spray from *my* nose.

We finished our breakfast with enough time to enjoy a few more cups of coffee and quite a bit more banter.

"You know, your parents have every right to be worried," I said.

"I'm an adult. I can take care of myself. I can't believe I felt like I had to ask permission in order to come on this trip. It is my decision whether I want to go out alone, with no escort to watch out for me. I should be able to go places alone, everyone else does and they are just fine."

"You *should* be able to. How about you take the first step and head on upstairs to the room and I'll meet you up there in a bit. We can change our clothes and get our massages," I suggested.

"Perfect, I'll meet you in ten?"

I nodded and she skipped off to the elevators. I finished my coffee and checked the time. I wanted to give her enough time for freedom, but not too much to where she might freak out because she was in a strange place alone.

I placed my empty mug down on the table and slipped out of the booth. Stepping up to the register, I signed the ticket to charge our meal to the room. After pulling the room key card from my purse, I headed over to the elevators and pressed the call button signaling I was going up.

As the elevator stopped, the light lit up over the doors of the one which had reached the lobby floor first. The doors split open and I stepped on pressing the button for the fourth floor.

Arriving at the door, sliding my key card into the slot, I opened the door.

"Give me five minutes to change into my yoga pants and a tank top then we can go," I said as I closed the door.

I walked over to the bed, opened my suitcase and pulled out my change of clothes. "Are you alright in there?" I asked Gwen through the closed bathroom door.

There was no answer as I changed outfits. I walked over and knocked on the door.

"Gwendolyn? Are you in there?" I turned the knob and immediately began picturing a bloody scene. The door opened all the way, but the room was empty. I checked behind the shower curtain, but nothing.

'Where could she have gone?' I wondered.

"Gwenie, this isn't funny. Where are you?" I said, my voice quivering.

Still no response. I began frantically searching the room. Unfortunately, the beds were on platforms so she couldn't hide under them and there was only one closet, but that was empty as well. She wasn't under the one table in the room either.

I even checked out on the balcony, but it was empty. That was it. I was out of places to look for her in the room.

I slipped my bare feet into my flip flops and headed back down to the lobby hoping we had just passed each other in the elevators.

'Maybe she came back to see if I was on my way up,' I wondered.

I walked over to the café and looked around. There was no sign of her. I walked over to the seating area in the lobby over by the front desk where we had checked in. She wasn't there either.

'Okay,' I thought. 'Maybe she got a boost of confidence in her new found freedom and decided she was going to go to the spa and wait for me there.'

I headed down the conference room hall to the spa. Just inside the door was a counter where the receptionist sat. On the wall to the right, were racks full of fashion magazines. To the left was a waiting area. There were three soft pink sofas set up like a square with only three sides. A small rectangular table was placed in the center with a table top waterfall placed in the center of that, as well as magazines circling the waterfall. Yet, still no Gwendolyn.

I stepped up to the counter and came face to face with a breathtakingly gorgeous young girl. Her skin was flawless and her shoulder length red hair had body and bounce, unlike my lifeless limp locks. I felt inferior to her.

"Hello, my name is Anjenette Marcum," I said in a quiet voice so as not to disturb the calming ambiance of the spa. "Has my friend Gwendolyn Welsh checked in for her massage yet?"

"No, I'm sorry," the woman whose name tag read 'Cathy' said. "She hasn't shown up. If the two of you don't check in within the next fifteen minutes, I'm going to have to bump you off the schedule." Her tone was harsh and rude, as if she didn't have time to answer frivolous questions.

Her name didn't match her attitude. I would have expected it to be Bonnie or Courtney with her 'I'm better than you' attitude. I no longer felt inferior.

"Thank you for your help and gratitude," I said sarcastically before turning to leave. I didn't have time to argue about the schedule. I went back out to the lobby.

"Excuse me," I said as I approached Spencer at the front desk.

"Hey girl," he greeted me. "What happened to your friend?"

"Have you seen her?" I inquired.

"Not since you checked in yesterday. She was feisty. I liked her. Did y'all get into a fight or something?" he pried.

"Or something," I replied. "Thank you Spencer."

I headed over to the café to see if maybe, just maybe, she had decided the joke was over and went back to find me. I asked the gentleman at the hosts stand if he had seen her.

"Not since she left earlier. Is something wrong?" he asked.

"I don't know yet," I said.

I decided to go back to the room and wait for her there. I was hoping she would be there waiting for me. When I opened the door and found it was still empty, my eyes welled up with tears.

Seven

I knew in order to file a police report Gwendolyn had to be missing for at least twenty four hours. She was an adult and had every right to disappear for as long as she wanted. I needed to have someone help me look for her, but I knew her mother would somehow figure out a way to blame me. So, I called my parents instead.

"Hello," my mother said in her cheery phone voice.

"Momma," I said, the way I always did when something was wrong.

"Anjenette? Is that you? What's wrong honey?" her tone changed to worried.

"Gwendolyn went missing this morning," I sobbed.

"What do you mean, missing? The two of you have only been gone one night."

"We were discussing her new found freedom at breakfast and I told her to take advantage of it while she could and to go up to the room and wait for me there, but when I got to the room she wasn't there and no one here at the hotel has seen her since she left the café."

"Okay, calm down. Have you called her mother?"

"Are you kidding? Doreen would kill me. What do you think I'm crazy?" I practically shouted into the phone.

"You know what, you're right. Doreen would blame you. She would say this is all your fault and try to find a way to make you feel worse about yourself than you already do right now. Your father and I will come to you. We will help you figure this out," my mother said, matter-of-factly.

"No, wait just a minute; this *is* my fault. I let her go alone. Maybe I *should* call Doreen and face my punishment now rather than later." I swiped at my nose with the back of my hand.

"Hold off on calling the Welshes until your father and I get there. The three of us can look together. If we don't find her by morning, then we will call the police and the Welshes." My mother hung up the phone without another word.

I lay on the bed, clutching my cell phone. I looked at the tiny electronic device in my grasp and smacked myself on the forehead with the palm of my hand.

"Why hadn't I thought of that before? Call Gwen's cell phone. Where it is, she is. She never goes anywhere without her phone. It is her only connection to the outside world, besides me," I said aloud to myself.

Since she hardly ever left the house, the few other friends she had, she kept in touch with them on the phone and through e-mails. Her phone was also her travel vlogger. It had the front facing camera so she could see herself while she recorded.

I went through my contacts list, found Gwen's number and pressed the call button. It rang.

After about five rings her voice mail picked up. I listened to her voice, "Hey, you've reached Gwen. Sorry I can't get to my phone right now because I'm at the beach. Ha, ha, yeah right. If you believe that you have the wrong number. Otherwise, leave me a message and I'll call you back. Bye!" I ended the call just before the beep tone sounded, indicating it would be recording a message and decided to retrace her steps calling her phone and listening for the ring tone.

I stepped out into the hallway, pressed the send button on my phone and called her again. As the phone rang, I walked down the hall toward the elevators, but only heard the ringing through my earpiece.

I ended the call then pressed the button on the wall to indicate I wanted to go downstairs. As the first elevator stopped in front of me and the doors opened, I pressed the call button on my cell again and listened for Gwen's ringtone. I stood in the doorway holding it open. Nothing. I stepped back and allowed the elevator to pass the floor. I pressed the button for the elevators again and waited. Each elevator that came to a stop at the fourth floor, the doors would opened and I would stand with my foot inside just enough to keep it from closing. After the last elevator came to a stop in front of me, I rode it down to the lobby, called the phone again, still with no luck.

I walked toward the café and pressed the call button on my phone again. I could hear a faint ring tone. I took each step carefully, slowly, toward the sound. The noise became louder as I got closer to the café. The tone stopped when her phone went to voicemail again.

I quickly ended the call and called her one more time. When I heard the tone again, I began walking until I was sure I was right next to it.

There was a potted tree standing next to me. I reached down into the pot and found her cell, discarded. I was positive then, something bad had happened to her. I held the devise in my left hand listening to the ring tone she had chosen. It was almost as though she had her own theme song. When the music stopped and I could hear her voice mail in my ear again, I let it play one more time before hanging up.

I took the phone up to the room and plopped down on the bed. After a few moments, I realized lying around wasn't going to help find Gwen. I had a notebook and pen in my suitcase, which I retrieved and began on the first floor of rooms.

I walked up and down each hallway writing down every room number. Someone had to have seen something. There was no way someone could be taken from a public place and not be seen. In order to be sure no one witnessed anything happen to Gwen, my plan was to question the other guests. I was going to wait until my parents arrived before speaking to anyone.

By the time I made it to the top floor, my cellular telephone was ringing. It was my mother.

"What room are you in?" she asked.

"Four oh two. Give me about five minutes and I'll meet you there." I hung up and finished writing the room numbers.

I headed back to my room to meet my parents. They were standing outside the door when I arrived. I was crying by the time I reached them. Both of them wrapped their arms around me. I allowed myself to cry for only a few more moments before wiping my face and letting them into the room.

My parents walked over and place their luggage on the bed furthest from the door, which is the bed Gwen chose. I began rifling through the pages of room numbers and splitting them up so each of us had four pages.

"What is this for?" my father asked.

"I wrote down every room number in the hotel so we could talk to each guest to see if anyone has seen Gwen. After we speak to the people in the room, you mark off whether they had seen her or not and when they saw her," I explained.

"That sounds like an organized way to talk to everyone. Considering it is the middle of the day, don't you think most people are going to be out sightseeing and such? Maybe we should come back to this later tonight. For now, let's go to lunch and we can hatch a plan," my mother suggested.

"I'm not hungry. Can we please just focus on looking for Gwen?" I said solemnly.

"Do you have a photo of her with you?" she asked me.

"I always do in case something like this was to happen. This is my fault. I should have never told her to go upstairs alone." Tears formed in the corner of my eyes and I immediately wiped them away.

"This is not your fault. How could you have known something like this would have happened?" my father said, placing a hand on my shoulder.

"You know Doreen is going to blame you enough for this. Don't torture yourself," my mother said in her calming, assertive tone. "Now, the first thing we need to do is take her picture around and ask the hotel staff if they have seen her. What time was it when you sent her upstairs?"

"About nine-thirty this morning. We had just enough time to come upstairs, change our clothes and head out to our massages," I explained as I pulled a tissue from the box on the night stand to blow my nose.

"Okay, first we can start by asking the staff at the café. Then we can ask at the front desk and the spa. If we come up empty handed, then we can go door to door asking guests if they have seen her," my mother planned.

"You really should eat something. You don't want to be hungry later when we are looking for Gwen," my father said.

"Really, I'm not hungry. Please, can we just go find Gwen? We need to focus on what is really important here."

Eight

My mother took the picture of Gwen and showed it around to the staff at the café.

"Have you seen this girl?" she asked a server.

"I saw her in here last night having dinner with her," he said as he pointed to me.

"Have you seen her today?"

"No, I'm sorry. I haven't seen her today."

"She had breakfast here this morning around seven and left around nine thirty, alone and hasn't been seen or heard from since."

"I'm sorry, I wish I could help you, but I only work the lunch shift today. I came in at eleven and will only be here until four when the dinner crew comes in."

"I appreciate you taking the time to talk to us. Here's my card. If you see her or hear anything, please call me." My mother pulled a type of business card out of her purse and handed it to the server.

"I sure will. I hope you find your friend," he said to me before walking to the back of the café.

"Well that was a bust and where did you get business cards? You don't have a job," I asked.

"You never know when you're going to need them. Suppose you meet someone interesting?" she said, touching the tip of my nose lightly with her index finger.

We walked over to the hosts stand and asked the young lady who was standing behind the podium.

"Have you seen this girl?" my mother asked her.

"I don't know. I see a lot of people every day. New day, new faces," she said.

"Well, you're not any help." My mother turned and walked toward the lobby with my father right behind her.

"I'm sorry. I don't think she meant to be rude," I explained to the hostess, as I followed my parents to the lobby.

She stopped next to the plant where I had found Gwen's phone. I looked down into the pot as my mother spoke, but I didn't hear a word she said. I was thinking about how things could have gone differently.

I was so intent on her being independent that I didn't think about how maybe Sterling was still stalking her. I couldn't even be sure Sterling was even behind this. Maybe she just decided she was tired of being babied and wanted to get out and explore the world around her. She was an adult who had never been out on her own. She never went anywhere alone and was always told what choices to make. Perhaps she made her own choice to ditch her cell phone and make a run for it to experience life alone.

"We need to get to a computer," I told them.

"What for?" my father asked.

"I want to check Gwen's vlog to see if she has posted anything new. Maybe we can find her that way," I explained.

It was just a theory, but I was keeping an open mind. We took off on a power walk to the front desk.

"Do you have a computer with an internet connection that we can use?" my mother asked the desk clerk.

"There is an internet café about two blocks from here," she explained. She reached under her computer, into a drawer and presented a brochure for the *Get Wired* internet café and coffee house.

"Thank you," I said as I grabbed the tri-fold and headed toward the front doors.

My mother grabbed my arm. "Slow down, honey. We are going to find her. You have to keep in mind that there may be nothing new. Don't get your hopes up just to have them come crashing down when what you hope for doesn't come true."

"Could you be just a little more optimistic? I'm the one who has to tell Doreen and Laird in the morning that we can't find their daughter." I pulled my arm free and continued on out the motion sensor automatic doors.

My parents talked amongst themselves behind me as I rushed down the side walk toward our destination. It was a little further than the desk clerk had told us, but the jaunt wasn't too bad. It actually gave me time to think. I needed the fresh air.

I approached the front door and paused for a moment to wait for my parents to catch up to me. I took a couple of deep soothing breaths then turned to face my mother and father.

"I know I may not find what I am looking for here, but I have to try. Gwen is my best friend and if something were to happen to her because of my lapse in judgment, I could never forgive myself." Before they could respond, I opened the door and stepped into the cyber world.

There was one table in the back not being occupied by someone, other than that, the place was packed full. I sat down and opened the laptop that was bolted to the table. The internet was already open on the screen. I moved the mouse up to the web browser and clicked on the web address to highlight it. I typed in Gwendolyn's vlog page website and pressed the enter key on the keyboard. I clicked on the vlog post that was dated one day before our vacation began.

She looked so happy as she talked about our trip. There was another post that had been uploaded two hours prior. I clicked on the new post.

"Hello all my fans out there in cyber land," she always began her vlog with the same phrase only this one had a sullen tone. "I am having fun on my mini vacation." Tears began to roll down her cheeks. "I promise to continue to update my vlog as much as possible, but I have decided to move." The staccato in her voice proved she was reading something.

"I have decided it is time for me to stop living in fear and start living more independently. To my family and friends, I'm sorry this is so sudden, but I need to do this in order to function properly in society since my mother…" she stopped and shook her head. Her eyes staring at the floor.

"Just say it," a voice in the background commanded. "Say it now or someone you love dies."

She sniffed hard, then continued, "Since my mother kept me sheltered most of my life and my best friend kept me locked indoors for the past few years." Her face was glistening from the light glaring off the moisture from the tears streaming down her face. "That is all for now. See you next time."

The video stopped. My parents were standing behind me peering over my shoulder. I was so angry. She looked terrified; I knew she was being forced to say those words. The voice off camera was undeniably Sterling's voice. Even my parents knew it. After what happened with Sterling the first time I vowed to take care of Gwen until she found someone to take over for me. I never wanted to see that look on her face again, yet there it was, staring back at me from the computer screen.

I moved the mouse to the top of the web page and clicked on the red X at the top right hand corner. I knew it was a long shot, but I had to try to believe I could save my friend.

I lowered the screen of the laptop and latched it to the base. My mother placed one hand on my shoulder.

"I understand you are upset Anjenette, but you have to take into account that this is not your fault. There was nothing you could have predicted," she told me.

"I just figured that after eight years she would have been safe. This doesn't make any sense. Why would he still be after her after all these years?" I asked.

"It doesn't have to make sense honey. No one knows why criminals do what they do. He could have been planning this move since the day he was paroled or even while he was incarcerated," my dad told me.

"You do realize that your words aren't helping any don't you?" I asked, looking up at him.

"I'm sorry. I just thought you would feel better knowing that there was nothing you could do to stop him if it was already planned out," he explained.

"I know. Let's just go back to the hotel and begin questioning the other guests. Maybe they saw what kind of car he was driving."

I was angry. Angry at myself for allowing her to be vulnerable and angry at Sterling for stewing all these years.

As I stood to leave, I saw a man staring in the front window at us. I didn't want to deal with it at the time. Mateo was now stalking me and I needed to find Sterling. I kept my eyes locked on his as I rushed to exit the building. A couple stood to leave and I almost bumped into them causing me to lose my focus on the watcher.

By the time we had made it out the door, he was gone.

Nine

We arrived back to the hotel with a little less hope. My mother walked up to the front desk to talk to the desk clerk.

"Do you have a guest staying here by the name of Sterling Bigum?" she asked.

"I'm sorry, but I can't give out that kind of information."

"Do you have security cameras around the hotel?"

"Yes we do. All throughout the lobby and café and there are two in every hallway," the clerk explained.

"Can we see the footage from this morning from right out in front of the café?" I asked, hopeful.

"Unless you are a member of law enforcement, you are not authorized to see them. If something has happened in the hotel to cause injury or harm, it should be reported to the authorities right away," the girl said.

"My friend went missing this morning and there isn't a police station in this world that would file a missing persons report if that person is an adult and hasn't already been missing for at least twenty four hours," I said with anger in my voice.

I felt helpless. There was nothing I could do to save my friend for the next eighteen hours. I didn't know how I was going to survive it. I walked over and plopped down in one of the chairs.

"This is all my fault," I yelled. "If I hadn't allowed her to go upstairs by herself she would still be here. I should have just put the kibosh on her whole plan of a vacation. I'm a lawyer. I should know how criminals think."

"You need to stop torturing yourself. This is not something you could have predicted. Wade, take her up to the room and see if you can get her to calm down while I check to see if I can get them to make me a couple copies of this picture of Gwen," my mother instructed my father.

Once we arrived back to the room, I began with other scenarios that Gwen and I could have done with the three day weekend to avoid the tragedy.

"We could have stayed home and played games or watched T.V. like we had been doing for the past three years that we have been living together," I screamed as I flung myself onto the bed.

I felt like a high school girl who had just had her heart broken by some boy. I didn't know what else to do. My best friend was missing and all I could think of doing was to throw a temper tantrum like a toddler. Had I completely lost it? I held my emotions back, sucked in a deep breath and sat up. I walked into the bathroom to compose myself.

Looking at myself in the mirror, I didn't even recognize the reflection that stared back at me. A wash cloth hung on the towel rack. Pulling it down from the bar, I turned on the hot water. I held the cloth under the water and rolled it around in my hands until the entire thing was drenched, hoping this would help me relax in order to think clearly.

Turning off the water and squeezing out as much of the moisture until the cloth was no longer dripping, I tilted my head back and draped it over my face. The warmth helped my muscles relax a little. Using it as an eraser, I swiped the cloth down my face, rubbing my eyes and wiping away the signs of sadness and anger. It was a situation I was unable to control.

I used the wash cloth to wipe my nose before discarding it on the counter and pulling a tissue from the dispenser and blowing my nose into it.

I again stared at my reflection while taking a few more deep breaths. Now I felt calm enough to return to the room with my father and act like an adult. I came out of the bathroom and my mother was now in the room as well.

"Are you feeling better now?" she asked.

"My best friend is missing and we have to find her," I said with an eerie calm in my voice.

"Okay, well, I had the desk clerk downstairs make copies of Gwen's photo so we all have one." My mother handed us each a copy of the picture along with the room lists. "When you knock on the door, if someone answers check it off. If no one answers write an X by the room number and we can go back to those rooms later.

"If anyone has seen her, write down the date and time she was spotted, if they say no, then write down the word no. Okay, let's go." My mother led the way out of the room and down the hall.

We stopped at the elevators and my mother pressed the arrow buttons to send her downstairs to the second floor and my dad and I were going up.

"We are going to meet back at the room in two hours whether we have finished our lists or not. Is everyone okay with that?" my mother asked.

"Let's just do this," I said as the elevator door opened.

The first one was going down. My mother stepped on and waived at us as the doors closed. The elevator behind us signaled its arrival. My father went up one floor and I went up five.

Before he stepped off the lift, my father hugged me. "Don't worry honey, we will find her no matter what," he whispered in my ear.

"Thank you daddy," I said.

He stood outside the elevator and watched as the doors closed. I didn't know how long he remained there, but I knew he was worried about me.

The elevator doors opened on the ninth floor and I stepped out. I looked down at the pages in my hand, took a deep breath and started with the first room to my right.

At the end of the two hours, I had almost made it to the end of my list. I only had one hallway left, but I knew it was time for a break. Only about one third of the rooms had anyone answer the door.

Unfortunately, no one I talked to had seen, or heard anything, nor had they even seen *her*. I stepped off the elevator onto the fourth floor and met my parents outside the room door.

"Any luck?" I asked as I approached.

"No, somehow she managed to slip away without anyone noticing," my father said, shrugging.

Ten

Once we were back inside the room, my mother decided to change her clothes. I followed suit by changing out of yoga pants and replacing them with pair of jeans and a T-Shirt.

"What are we doing now?" I asked.

"I noticed a bunch of shops earlier when we were going to the internet café and coffee house. Most of them don't open until five. Since we were able to kill some time, I figure we could walk around and visit some of the places outside," my mom said.

"Are you kidding me?" I yelled at her. "Gwendolyn is missing, possibly kidnapped and you want to go shopping?"

"No Anjenette, not shopping. I just thought that if Gwen went out on her own, that maybe *she* would want to go shopping. We could go in a few places and ask if they had seen her," she recovered.

"And if in the process you pick up something for you it's just a bonus, right?" I could feel the rage build up inside me.

"Really Carrie Ann? Is it appropriate for you to want to go shopping right now?" my father said to my mother.

"Besides that, mother, Gwen was excited to go to the spa. I doubt she would ditch me to go shopping. The whole situation reeks of Sterling," I explained. "Not only that, but if you listen to your words, you just said the shops don't open until five. If she has been missing since nine thirty this morning, how could she have been spotted at a place that didn't open until seven and a half hours after she came up missing?"

"Maybe he grabbed her and walked around outside the shops to blend in with the crowd so as not to get caught," she said.

"Maybe he grabbed her and immediately stuffed her into his car and they are already out of the state," I argued.

The altercation that occurred in the parking garage at my office with Mateo immediately came flooding to mind. *Could it be possible,* I thought. *Maybe Mateo was the culprit behind Gwen's disappearance in order to get to me. He did tell me to watch my back. Perhaps I was the next to be abducted. Maybe I was mistaken who the male voice belonged to.*

"I might be the next victim in this family for tragedy to strike," I told my parents.

"What are you talking about?" my father asked.

I told them about the incident with Mateo and hoped my mother wouldn't overreact.

"He could be the voice in the background of her vlog. This may be his way to get back at me," I explained.

"Why didn't you tell us this before?" my mother chastised.

"I figured I could handle him on my own. Plus, the law states that verbal threats don't count, he actually has to physically harm me in some way in order for the police to do anything," I explained.

"Well now that doesn't seem right," my father complained.

"Technically, he threatened you with a gun. And you said he shot it above your car. Doesn't that count?" my mother wondered.

"I spoke to the partners at work and we were able to get him arrested and charged, but he only spent four days in jail. I was able to obtain a temporary restraining order, but Mateo doesn't seem like the kind of person to follow what a piece of paper says. My only fear is, if he took Gwen, I could be next." I knew what he was capable of. I saw the pictures of what he had done to my client. I could only imagine what he would do if he got his hands on another victim.

"If he told *you* to watch *your* back, why would he go after Gwen?" my father asked.

"If he would threaten me, why wouldn't he take Gwen just to make my life miserable," I assumed.

"If he wanted to make your life miserable, don't you think he would have done something specifically to you? I think we should stick with the Sterling theory seeing as he has held her against her will before," my father explained.

"I'm positive that is Sterling's voice in her video too. I recognized that voice. If it belong to this Mateo fellow, I wouldn't be sure, but I am sure it is Sterling," my mother interjected.

"I think that when we talk to the cops in the morning, we should give them both names just in case," I said.

"Well, let's head out so we can get back in time for dinner," my mother commented.

"Are you still planning to go out shopping?" I asked.

"Not shopping. I figured we could show the street vendors her picture and find out if they have perhaps seen her. I'm going whether you want to or not." My mother started for the door.

"Fine," I said reluctantly.

The three of us headed out of the hotel. We walked up and down the streets showing random people the copy of Gwen's picture. I clung to my dad afraid I was being watched.

After about an hour and probably one hundred no's, we headed back to the hotel, frustrated.

"I can't believe we have to sit around and wait. I want my friend back," I yelled.

"I know you do honey, but look at it this way, if we don't find her, at least when we go home you won't have anyone to take care of except yourself. You can finally have a normal life and get married," my mother suggested.

Her comment was causing me to suspect she was behind Gwen's disappearance somehow. I now had three suspects in mind and I couldn't believe one of them was my mother.

"Maybe you should stop talking right now," I told her.

"I'm just saying, I think she has held you back all these years from having any kind of relationship with a man. This could be one of those blessings in disguise," she explained.

"Shut up! Shut up! Shut up! Have you ever thought that maybe I was in a relationship with Gwen? Her friendship meant more to me than any relationship with a man could. Now, one more comment about this and I'm calling the police right now and telling them I saw *you* murder Gwen and have you arrested."

"Who said anything about murder? Until we find Gwen, we should assume she is still alive," my father pointed out.

"The way she is talking, we could only assume Gwen is never coming back," I stated.

"We all just need to relax," my mother said.

I sat down on the bed and pulled out my notebook and pen. "Today was pretty much a waste of time. We need to hash out a plan for tomorrow. I will have to contact Doreen and Laird and explain to them I lost their daughter. I will also more than likely receive a tongue lashing from Doreen. I need to prepare myself for that."

My father decided it was time to shut it down. "I think that we should get a good night's rest. We are all tired and cranky. In the morning we can do our morning rituals and call the police to report Gwendolyn missing. Once the report is made, then and only then, do we contact her parents to inform them about their daughter. Anjie, I think you should be the one to tell them."

"You know Doreen is going to blame me, as she should. This is my fault. I should have never let her go to the room alone." I rubbed my face with my hands as tears welled up in my eyes.

"This is not your fault, sweetheart," my mother comforted.

"I'm sorry about what I said before," I told her. "I didn't mean it."

"No, I'm sorry. I should have never said those things. I just feel like Gwen is holding you back from experiencing life the way it is meant to be lived. You never think about you and your needs, it is always her and her needs. I just wish you would date a little. I would like to have grandchildren someday."

"Oh yeah, that is exactly what I want to do. I want to go into a dark restaurant with someone I know nothing about and spend hours talking and having a good time with a man that could potentially snap one day and hold me hostage. I want to be tied up and held against my will until the police rescue me. That sounds great," I said, sarcastically.

"See, that is exactly what I am talking about. Because of Gwen and what happened to her, you are afraid to go out and date like normal people. Have you ever gone out with friends from work?" my mother asked, sounding concerned.

"As soon as my day is over, I have to get home to Gwen. If I don't get home by seven she calls me in a panic. I have to listen to her rant about how worried she was and if I wasn't going to be home on time I should have called so she could have made arrangements with her mother to come over and sit with her until I got home. How can I do anything else? My life consists of work and home and that is it. I have accepted it and you should too."

"That is my point Anjie. Your whole life revolves around Gwen. Now unless the two of you plan on adopting little Chinese babies together, you need to live your own life and stop worrying so much about a grown woman."

"You just don't get it, do you? I have agreed to live my life this way to keep Gwen safe. I would rather take care of her and make sure she is alive and happy, than go to my best friend's funeral because some asshole decided to take her from this world. Now then, if you don't mind, I have to figure out what I am going to say to her parents."

I stood and pulled the covers back on the bed. Climbing in and laying down, I pulled my knees up and placed the notebook on my lap in order to write. No matter how much my mother aggravated me I still loved her. I wasn't in the mood to deal with her and her ranting's of how I had wasted my life taking care of a grown woman instead of having children to take care of. I began writing a script as to what to say to Gwen's parents when I called. We all knew we were going to have a long exhausting day ahead of us.

Eleven

I had a hard time sleeping knowing that Gwendolyn was out there somewhere possibly terrified. If I fell asleep for even just a minute, I dreamt of all the horrible things that could have happened to Gwen.

I drifted off about one a.m. and my subconscious mind went to a disturbing place. It was as though I were there, watching as she was raped, repeatedly. She was crying and her face was bruised from being beaten. One eye was swollen shut and there was a laceration on the lower lid of that eye that was oozing thick yellow fluid.

When he had decided he was done with her, he took a wavy edged paring knife and disemboweled her. Sliced her open from hip to hip. My body was stiff. I tried to run to her, but couldn't move. I could only watch as her intestines oozed from her abdomen. My focus turned to her face as her head turned to look at me. Her eyes were wide open without any signs of life left in them. She opened her mouth and shouted, 'Save me Anjenette'.

I jolted awake, covered in sweat. I rolled over and glanced at the clock on the bed side table. Four a.m. I refused to close my eyes in fear of seeing more images of Gwen being tortured.

I sat up and peered over at the bed Gwen had slept in our first night. My mother and father lay sleeping peacefully.

I got out of bed and went into the bathroom to shower and dress for the day ahead.

When I came out of the bathroom, my father was sitting at the table, but my mother continued to sleep. Once he noticed me standing there, he stood and ushered me out the door into the hallway.

"What's going on?" I asked him.

"You know, your mother is just worried about you. She thinks that because you have elected to take care of Gwen, you don't have enough time to take care of yourself and live your own life. She just wants what's best for you," he said.

"Some of the things she said last night were very hurtful. I think of Gwen as a sister and for mom to say that this situation is a blessing in disguise was as if to say that my sister was a burden. I love her and know that someday she will be ready to be on her own and when that day comes, I will be there to support her."

"You need to keep in mind that we may never find Gwen alive. Let's go for a walk."

I stepped back into the room and grabbed my clutch from the dresser. I took one last look at myself in the mirror before rejoining my father in the hallway.

"I understand that Gwen may no longer be among the living, but I don't want to think about it," I said as we approached the elevators.

"It may be something you will have to consider."

My father pressed the button to call the elevator. Luckily it didn't take long to arrive. We stepped on and I starred at my feet.

"Dad, I really do think of Gwen like my sister and you and Mom have always treated her like part of the family, so I don't understand why she would speak ill of a member of the family like that," I said as the elevator stopped and the doors opened.

"Your mother means well," my father said as we walked through the lobby of the hotel.

"I'm sure she does, but she really should choose her words more carefully," I replied.

As we exited the hotel, the cool breeze of the early morning was a nice change to the smoldering heat of the day. The humidity in the air caused my skin to feel sticky and I could smell the moisture. Luckily it was only May and the Texas heat was bearable. The restaurants that served breakfast where open and the aroma of eggs, pancakes, toast and cinnamon rolls emitted through the open doors as patrons entered and exited as they started their day.

"I will talk to her."

"Thank you. I need your support, not your criticism and I don't want to feel as though I have to go at this alone and send the two of you home because she can't be nice."

"Once we get back to the hotel I will make sure she is only supportive and no longer critical."

I stopped and turned to face him. "I love you, Dad," I said as I wrapped my arms around him in an embrace.

We walked down passed the internet café and noticed they were open. I stopped in front of the doors and turned to my father.

"Can we go in for just a moment? I want to see if anything new has been posted," I requested.

"You can't make yourself crazy like this. We can go in, but it will only be for the coffee," he replied.

We stepped inside to an enveloping scent of cappuccinos and freshly roasted coffee beans. We glanced over the menu array of different flavors. It was still fairly early, but the coffee house appeared as though it was late afternoon. Some people strolled in looking like zombies until their first sip of liquid energy.

"I'll take a caramel mocha coffee," I told my father, as we waited in line. "I'm going to run to the bathroom for a moment."

"Anjenette, please don't make this any harder than it already is," my father said, as I stepped away from him.

I pretended not to hear him as I made my way to a back corner table to hide. I lifted the screen of the lap top that was bolted to the table and it immediately illuminated.

I moved the little arrow up to the search bar and searched for Gwen's vlog. When the page appeared, I scanned over the entire screen hoping for something new. Unfortunately, it was still early and the last posting made was the one she had been forced to record.

I exited the page and lowered the screen. As I stood up from the table my father was headed toward me, coffee in hand and disappointment on his face.

"What did I tell you?" he chastised.

"I know, but I had to look," I told him, tears glistening in my eyes.

"Come on, let's get back before your mother wakes up. I got some coffee for her too and I don't want it to get cold."

He draped his arm around my shoulders and we walked back to the hotel in silence.

By the time we made it back, it was seven in the morning and my mother was sitting at the table reading. She was waiting for us to get back.

"Where did the two of you go off to this morning?" she asked.

"For a walk," my father answered.

"You didn't think to ask if I wanted to go?"

"It was a walk to clear our heads and to discuss the harsh conversation from last night."

My mother stood, walked over in front of me and placed her hands on my shoulders. "Anjenette, you know I didn't mean what I said with the way it came out, don't you?"

I reached up and touched her hands. "You may not have meant it the way you said it, but you have to realize that Gwen is not only my best friend, she is like a sister to me. I need her as much as she needs me."

Just then Gwendolyn's phone rang. The three of us froze, not knowing what to do. We stared at the electronic device as if it were a snake reared up and ready to strike. I thought it could be Gwen, but then I thought it could be her mother. I wasn't ready to tell Doreen her daughter was missing.

I finally reached over and picked the phone up off the night stand and peered at the caller ID on the screen. "Holy shit! It's Doreen. Maybe if I don't answer it she will think we are still sleeping and wait an hour to call back. By then I can have a story made up of what Gwen is doing and why she can't come to the phone." I thought my plan was brilliant when the ring tone stopped making noise.

"Doesn't Doreen and Laird have a step by step schedule of your activities?" my mother pointed out, then Gwen's phone rang again.

I sighed heavily before answering Gwen's phone as happy as I could. "Hello," I said in a sing song way.

"Anjenette? Where is Gwendolyn?" Doreen made it abundantly clear she did not want to talk to me.

"She's not here for the moment."

"Well, where is she? She shouldn't be alone. Why aren't you supervising her?"

"Look Doreen, first of all, Gwen is a grown woman and if she wants to go somewhere alone, she is allowed," I griped.

"Where is my daughter Anjenette?" Doreen sounded aggravated with a hint of fear.

I decided to just blurt it out. "I don't know. Yesterday morning she…" I told her everything that had transpired the previous day.

There was silence on the other end of the line. I wasn't sure if she had hung up on me, or if she had passed out from shock.

"Doreen?" I said and heard the click of the call being disconnected. "She hung up on me," I said staring at the phone.

"Call the police and report her missing. You know Doreen and Laird are on their way," my mother said.

I used the hotel room phone to call the police. First, I called down to the lobby to acquire the number to the police station.

"Sundaisy sheriff's office," a female voice came through the phone.

"I need to report a missing person," I told the dispatcher.

"Adult or child?"

"Adult," I said as I listened to her tap away on a keyboard.

"Has this person been missing for at least twenty four hours?"

"Yes ma'am, and several years ago she was held captive for three days by a man who was recently released from prison."

"Do you believe this is the person who is responsible for her disappearance?"

"Of course I do, otherwise I wouldn't have mentioned it."

"All right ma'am, calm down. I will dispatch an officer to your location. I see you are calling from The Rizzy Hotel and Spa is that correct?"

"Yes ma'am. I am in room four oh two."

"A patrol car is on the way."

I disconnected the phone call. The only thing we had left to do was wait, again.

Two hours later we heard arguing on the other side of the door.

"What are you doing to try to find my daughter?" a female voice shouted.

I knew immediately it was Doreen yelling at an officer. I walked over and snatched the door open.

"Doreen, so nice of you to join us. Please, come in," I said, as I stepped aside to allow Doreen, Laird and two uniformed officers in the room.

"I'm Deputy Samuels and this is Deputy Roth," one officer introduced, as they entered the room.

Doreen immediately started accusing me as soon as the door latched.

"How could you let this happen? It was reckless and irresponsible. You should have known better than to allow her to wander off alone." She stood so close to me I could smell the stagnant scent of coffee on her breath.

"Doreen, I couldn't have predicted…"

"Anjenette, you should have thought about it. You're a smart girl, but this was dumb on your part," she cut me off.

"Now wait just a minute. That is a harsh thing to say. There was no way of knowing something like this would happen," my mother interjected.

"Maybe the two of you are in this together!" Doreen shouted.

"You are out of line!" I shouted back.

"You told her to go alone so your mother could get rid of her for you." Doreen shoved me and I bounced down onto the bed I had been sleeping in.

"You Bitch!" I sprang into a standing position, nose to nose with Doreen.

One sheriff's deputy grabbed ahold of me and the other grabbed Gwen's mother, but I continued to defend myself to her.

"I love Gwenie like a sister! She is part of my family and no matter what shit falls out of your mouth, I will never stoop to physical violence with you because Gwenie always wanted us to get along," I said through clenched teeth.

"Are you ladies done so we can do our job or would the two of you like to hash it out in a holding cell for a few hours?" Deputy Samuels ask, as he loosened his grip on me.

"I'm done," I said, as I sat on the end of the bed closest to the door, facing the balcony.

"Come along Doreen. Let's have a seat and talk to the nice police officers," Laird said, as he led her to the table by the sliding glass door.

My parents joined me on the bed. Doreen and Laird sat at the table on the other side of the room and the two deputies sat on the other bed between us. One officer pulled out a small notebook.

"So, who is who here?" Officer Roth asked.

"I'm Doreen, Gwendolyn's mother. This is her father Laird. The other three don't matter."

"Who called to make the report?"

"That would be me. I'm Anjenette, Gwen's best friend. These are my parents, Carrie Anne and Wade. Gwen and I came here for a spa weekend."

"Exactly, this is your fault," Doreen interrupted. "If you wouldn't have convinced her to come here, she would be safe at home."

"Like I told you before, this was her idea. I didn't have to convince her, she came running."

Twelve

"Why don't you start from the beginning? When did you arrive?" Roth asked.

"It was Friday afternoon, about three," I answered.

"Did you do anything?"

"When we first arrived it was too early to check in so we looked around the hotel for a little while. After we checked in, we went down to the pool and out to the sun deck. We came back upstairs and changed to go to dinner at the lobby restaurant. After that we just came back to the room and watched T.V. until we fell asleep."

"Did you notice anyone watching her?"

"I wasn't really paying attention. We were focused on each other and excited to be relaxing."

"When did you notice she had disappeared?" Roth continued.

"After she had forced my sweet Gwendolyn to come up to the room alone, knowing something bad was going to happen," Doreen interjected.

"I had no way of knowing that. She was the one who made the decision to go by herself. She noticed the ridiculousness of having to ask your permission to go on this trip considering the fact that she is an adult," I explained.

"Can we please get back on track so we can find your friend and your daughter?" Samuels asked, motioning at me then the Welshes. "What time did she leave to come up to the room?"

"It was about nine thirty yesterday morning. We had just had breakfast downstairs in the hotel restaurant."

"Can you tell me what she was wearing the last time you saw her?" Roth asked.

"She had on a purple top with jeans. No, wait. She was coming up to the room to change her clothes so she might be wearing her black yoga pants," I informed.

"So you don't know what your friend was wearing?" Samuels more stated, rather than asking.

"Is there anyone you can think of who would want to hurt her?" Roth said, ignoring Samuels comment.

"Years ago her high school boyfriend, Sterling Bigum, held her hostage," I replied.

"You believe this Sterling Bigum has come back for her?" Deputy Roth asked, as he jotted down notes in his notebook.

"He is the only one who could have. Gwendolyn hasn't left the house alone since he was paroled," I told them.

"Is there any proof that he could be the one responsible?" Deputy Samuels asked.

"The hotel has cameras, but we weren't allowed to view them," I explained.

"We will take a look at the videos and interview this Sterling Bigum. If you have any questions or would like to add any more information to the report, please let us know." Samuels handed each of us a card. "If we have any other questions, we will contact you."

I stood and walked Roth and Samuels to the door. As they exited, Doreen immediately started in on me again. She stood and walked over to me. "This is your fault. You brought her here, you told her to go off by herself. You should be arrested."

"Doreen that is enough. Gwendolyn is a grown woman. She should be able to take care of herself," Laird told her.

"I was trying to help her. I would never intentionally put her in harm's way." I felt my face flush with anger as I defended myself.

"And yet here we are. My daughter is missing because you *did* put her in harm's way. What are you going to do now?" Doreen was inches away from my nose.

"I think we should contact the news stations and tell them what happened with Gwendolyn and see if they can run a story so people can be on the lookout for her," my mother suggested.

"What about Sterling? Shouldn't we warn people about him?" Doreen said.

"Technically no one saw the abduction. You can't accuse someone of something they may not have had anything to do with."

"I think we should set up a stake out and while the ladies are talking to the news stations and newspapers, we can look out for anyone suspicious," my father said to Laird.

"I think the three of you are done here. Laird and I can handle this from now on," Doreen suggested.

"I'm not leaving until I find out what happened to my friend," I said as I picked up the pen and notebook. I sat on the bed next to my mother. "Now, what should we say to the media?"

"Oh, yes you are. I want you gone. I think you have done enough damage." Doreen opened the door to the room and motioned us to leave.

"You have some nerve. I'm the one who has to live with the guilt of this tragic situation and all you can do is think about yourself. My best friend went missing on my watch. That means I am determined to find out what happened to her and no one is going to stop me," I informed her.

"You should feel guilty. You are the reason my little girl is gone. If anyone is going to talk to the news media it is going to be her grieving mother," Doreen stated.

"Grieving? You make it sound like she is dead and you're pleading with the public to help find her killer rather than her kidnapper. You're a real piece of work, you know that. I am trying to find someone who is still very much alive and you already want to write her off as being dead. Some mother you are. Maybe you had something to do with her disappearance and that is why you say she is dead." I was outraged by her lack of positivity.

"Are you kidding me right now? You are the reason we are all here. You are the reason she is missing. I want you gone, all three of you. I am taking over from here." Doreen's face heated into a shade of crimson and she balled up her fists.

I stood from the bed and moved toward Doreen. Taking one step at a time closer to her hoping she would hit me. "Go ahead Doreen. You know you want to. Just make it count," I encouraged.

"Doreen, you need to calm down. We are here for Gwendo-lyn. Just keep your focus on finding her," Laird said, as he placed his hands on her shoulders.

Doreen turned toward Laird and practically collapsed into his arms. She began to cry uncontrollably and could barely stand on her own. Laird led her over to a chair at the table and helped her into a seated position. He knelt down in front of her.

"My baby girl, my only child is gone, without a trace and none of you seem to care about my feelings," Doreen said.

"You are making it sound more like you are the victim here instead of Gwen. You know what? I think it would be easiest if you left. We can find her without your selfishness," I said.

I turned toward my parents so my back was now facing Doreen. I couldn't even look at her.

"So how do you set up a press conference for this kind of thing?" My mother asked.

"I guess we could just call all the news stations and give them a statement about what happened and they could do the rest. They are the pros at this kind of thing. Maybe they would help and ask questions," I suggested.

"That sounds like a good idea and everything, but what if they don't take you seriously? If that is the case, they won't even air your story and we would be wasting precious time sitting around when we could be out there looking for her," Doreen said from across the room.

I ignored her comment and continued focusing on my parents. "Maybe I should just write down everything I know about Gwen, her personality, the way she walks and talks. You know stuff like that."

"What good is that going to do? That doesn't say anything about what happened to her," Doreen interjected again.

"Honey, Anjenette could be useful for this. She was the last person to see our daughter and she's a lawyer. She can be ruthless and pushy to make sure the media listens," Laird reassured Doreen.

"Write down everything about the last time you saw her," Doreen said, finally on board with the idea.

As I jotted down every detail of the morning before, we were startled by a knock on the door. The five of us exchanged glances. Laird stood and walked over to open the door.

Two sharply dressed men, along with an attractive female, stood on the other side of the threshold. They introduced themselves as FBI.

"Good afternoon, I'm Agent Henry Jarvis with the FBI. This is Agent Donald Fleck and Agent Elizabeth Herring. May we come in?" one gentleman introduced as they produced their government badges.

"Why would the FBI be investigating a disappearance?" my mother asked as Laird moved aside to allow them to enter the room.

"We are here investigating another case. The local police have asked us to assist in locating your friend since you seem to be sure it is more than just a missing person case. The FBI steps in on abduction cases," Agent Fleck explained.

"Abduction? That makes it sound violent. What is the case you are here investigating about?" my mother asked.

"Well, that's classified information ma'am," Agent Herring stated.

"Classified or not, if you think something has happened to my daughter, I want to know what it is," Doreen insisted.

"We just wanted to ask you a few questions to possibly eliminate her disappearance as being connected to the case," the FBI agent who introduced himself as Henry Jarvis said.

"I can tell you this much, we did a search on this Sterling Bigum guy and all we came up with was his arrest and parole dates. Shortly after that he just disappears. There is no bank information, no credit cards, no housing. Nothing with that name on it," agent Herring pointed out.

"What about his parole officer? Doesn't he have to report to him every so often?" I asked.

"We are looking into it, but so far Bigum only reported to him three times since his release. A warrant was issued, but like I said, he just disappeared," Herring explained.

"How does someone just disappear?" I stood, enraged.

All three of the government agents stood as well and each placed their hands on their guns. I put my hands up in a surrender motion and sat back down, slowly.

"I understand the line of work you're in causes you to be paranoid, but gees, calm down." I placed my hands down on my knees.

"We are trained to be prepared for anything," Agent Fleck said as the three of them returned to their seats.

"Has Gwendolyn ever mentioned feeling as though she was being followed?" Agent Herring asked.

"She never leaves the house alone. Someone is always with her," I said.

"She could still be followed even if she was with someone else," Herring explained.

"If she did feel that way, she never said anything to me," I told her.

"Did she ever look around while the two of you were out? Possibly like she was looking for someone?" Fleck inquired.

"I don't know. I can't remember. I'm a horrible friend. I can't even remember if my best friend felt like she was being followed, or watched," I told them, staring at my lap.

"That doesn't make you a horrible friend. You have to remember though, her mother had ingrained her with irrational fears. If she normally looked around and was always checking over her shoulder, you may not have noticed because you were used to seeing it," my mother said.

"That's right. She had done that all the time. For as long as I can remember, Gwen was always looking over her shoulder, telling me people were watching her. One time in high school, she told me her mother said there was a killer on the loose who killed teenage girls that had premarital sex and she thought he was at our school because there were so many harlots walking the halls. When I asked her if she was worried he was going to get her, she told me she was afraid he might make a mistake and kill her instead. Another time, when we were in fifth grade, Doreen told her there was a satanic cult running amuck on the streets taking little girls for sacrifice. She told me she was sleeping in her parents' room." I shot Doreen a condescending look.

"Did she tell you how long she stayed in their room?" Herring asked.

"I think it was almost a month before Laird actually explained the whole story to her," I said.

"Which was?" Herring pried.

"Yes, there was a group of hooligans running around tagging random houses with red spray paint. The news said it could be gang related and Doreen turned the story into ritualistic sacrificing. Gwendolyn never stood the chance of a normal life growing up with an overbearing mother. Poor thing was always looking over her shoulder," my mother interjected.

"Mrs. Welsh, do you realize that scaring your child into believing the world is evil is considered as a form of mental abuse? To top it all off, evil things have actually happened to her. In this case she has been held hostage by her boyfriend and now she has been abducted by an unknown assailant, which is assumed is the same man from the first incident. If you had raised her like any normal parent, she would have known how to handle these situations rather than putting herself in the situation in the first place out of defiance of her overbearing mother," Jarvis lectured.

My jaw dropped. I couldn't believe he had the balls to say what everyone was thinking, but knew better than to say out loud. I looked over in Doreen's direction. Her face was turning bright red and I thought her head might explode.

"So, how did Sterling disappear?" my mother asked, wide eyed, before Doreen had time to blow up.

"Being an ex-con he may have had some connections to some people for help with that," Herring answered.

"We are still trying to locate him. We have reason to believe he may have changed his name," Agent Jarvis stated.

"Who the hell do you think you think you are? Questioning a mother on her parenting." Doreen finally spoke and stood. "You go out there every day and see the evil in this world and you have the unmitigated gall to lecture me about my parenting skills. How dare you," she said, slowly stepping toward Jarvis.

"Just calm down, Mrs. Welsh. You know everyone here was thinking it," Jarvis justified his actions.

"And yet, you were the only one to voice your opinion. At least the rest of these people know the definition of the word tact. I have known the Marcums for years and never once have they ever been as rude to me as you have been in the last few minutes. I hope you rot in hell you bastard," Doreen said, before stepping into the bathroom and closing the door.

No one at that point knew what to say. We exchanged a few glances. The looks on everyone's faces expressed fear for being the first to speak.

"We were thinking of calling a press conference to see if maybe she is out there somewhere, to plead for her to come back to us or if we could at least be contacted so we know what happened," my mother broke the silence.

"That might actually be a good idea. We will have our agent in charge of coordinating that have it all set up for you when it is time," Fleck said.

"What do we do in the mean time?" I asked.

"Have lunch and wait for our call."

"We can't just sit around and wait. We need to do something now. I know time is critical in an abduction case," I said.

"For now, there is nothing you can do," Jarvis stated as the agents stood and headed for the door.

"Agents, please let us know if you hear anything. And Agent Jarvis, you should really learn to think before you speak," Doreen said peeking out the bathroom door.

The agents departed, which also left us frustrated and confused. They were there investigating an unrelated case, but somehow felt it was imperative to ask questions about Gwen's disappearance. If it was that unrelated, why were they also trying to find Sterling when he was suspect number one on *our* list?

Doreen emerged from the bathroom and joined us. She sauntered over to the table near the balcony and sat down quietly.

I wrote down a few questions I was going to answer by doing my own investigation. No one was really hungry enough to eat nor did any of us want to. I picked up the remote to the television and turned on the news.

Thirteen

The news reporter was standing in front of a ranch style home with a well-manicured lawn. As soon as he was introduced, he stood up straighter and cleared his throat.

"Thank you Cindy. I'm standing in front of a home, where early yesterday morning, police found a gruesome scene. The remains of fifteen people were found throughout the home. Each body had been preserved through a form of taxidermy.

"The house is registered to a man named Theodore Ramirez. An investigation has determined Ramirez is an alias, but the true identity hasn't been determined as of this morning.

"Local police have called for help in the investigation from the FBI in locating the home owner. We will have more on this story coming up at six and ten. This is Tom Zane for investigation news two. Back to you Cindy."

"Now Tom, you said the bodies were in a state of taxidermy?"

"Yes Cindy. The victims had been cut open as in an autopsy and their internal organs removed. Some had been stuffed with a wooden torso, others with an expanding spray foam. Each victim was posed throughout the house as though each had their own role to play. The names of the victims aren't being released until the families are contacted."

"I don't want that phone call," Doreen said, sobbing.

"If the house was abandoned, there's no way Gwendolyn is there. She hasn't been missing long enough to be left in an abandoned house," my mother said.

"Maybe we should go talk to the neighbors around this Theodore Ramirez's house and see if we can't get a description of him. If the name is an alias and Sterling is in hiding, it could be him," I suggested.

"That's a great idea, Anjie. The only problem is we don't know where the house is located," Doreen said condescendingly.

"We could go to the police station, talk to the FBI and see if they will give us that information or if we could go with them to talk to the neighbors. Either way, we could convince them we want to help," I said.

"Of course, because the police enjoy it so much when civilians get in the way of their investigations," Doreen rolled her eyes and turned in her chair in order to look out the window.

"Considering we know what he looks like and his mannerisms, we actually could help," I told her.

"You do what you want; I'm going to find my daughter." Doreen stood and left the room.

"Laird, why don't you go with Doreen to keep her safe? Wade can stay here incase Gwendolyn walked off on her own and she decides to come back here. Anjenette and I are going down to the police station and see if we can get any information about this Theodore Ramirez," my mother said.

Laird nodded then left to be with Doreen and my mother and I headed over to the police station. Since each officer and FBI agent we spoke to had given us their card, we were able to line up a list so we could speak to at least one of five people. On the ride over to the station I put the cards in order of who we would prefer to talk to first.

Agent Herring seemed to be the most sympathetic. Agent Fleck was quiet. He seemed as though he would be willing to listen to our suggestions. Agent Jarvis was a pompous ass. He was my last resort, right after Officer Roth and Officer Samuels. My only hope was to get help from law enforcement to bring Gwen home safe.

When we arrived at the station, my mother pulled into a parking space then turned to face me. I started to open the passenger door to exit the vehicle and she placed her hand on my arm.

"Anjie, what if we don't find what you are looking for? What if this is some other crazy maniac and it turns out to be a false lead? Even if Theodore Ramirez turns out to be Sterling, we can't even be sure he is behind her disappearance," she said.

"It doesn't hurt to try," I responded.

"I understand that, but you prosecute these cases on a daily basis. You know how many nut jobs are out there. Please don't put all your hope on this case thinking this is the one. Maybe Gwen just ran off hoping to get away from her neurotic mother. In which case you should be following her vlog instead of a possible dead end lead."

"I don't care how many times I have to go through this, Mom. I am going to find Gwen no matter how I have to do it."

I opened the car door and got out. After closing it, I stood outside the vehicle taking deep breaths. I closed my eyes and imagined Gwen's smiling face to help muster up the strength to fight back the tears. I had to be strong for Gwen.

My mother came around the front of the car and touched my shoulder. I opened my eyes and took one more deep breath. I swallowed back the lump in my throat and we continued up the stairs to the doors to the police station.

"Let's go," I said.

I pulled open the door to the station and headed up to the police officer behind the counter in a small vestibule area. Along the wall to the right was a row of four wooden chairs and to the left was another doorway.

"Excuse me," I said to the officer. "We are looking for FBI agent Elizabeth Herring. We believe we have some information that may be useful in the case of Theodore Ramirez."

"Can I get your names?" She asked.

"My name is Anjenette Marcum and this is my mother Carrie Anne."

"Can I ask what the information is?" she asked as she wrote our names on a legal sized yellow note pad.

"I would prefer keeping the information confidential. We're only going to tell Agent Herring." I fake smiled at the officer.

She nodded and picked up the phone on the desk in front of her. "Please have a seat," she said, motioning toward the row of chairs.

The officer pressed a couple of numbers into the phone and turned so her back faced us. I knew it was her way to try and muffle her voice so we couldn't hear the phone call. I used that move plenty of times when I answered my phone while interviewing witnesses for a case - especially when they were witnesses for the defense. It also helped to turn around, look at them once during the call and say 'hmmm'. They automatically assume I learned some more information and once I hung up they would offer information. I focused my hearing intently on her phone conversation.

"I have a couple of ladies here wanting to speak to agent Herring." She said, then listened for a response.

"Carrie Anne and Anjenette Marcum. They say they have information regarding the Theodore Ramirez case." She nodded, as if the person on the other end of the line could see her. She used the move and turned around to glance at us, turned back around then hung up.

She turned her focus back to us and said, "Agent Herring will be right up to get you."

What did she mean by 'up'? I wondered. I thought that was something that was said when someone was traveling from the south to the north. I just assumed she was one of those people who have no sense of direction so when you ask where they are going they say 'up the street' when in fact the street has no elevation to it at all and technically there is no up or down.

After a few moments of thought and considering the officer would have been more accurate to say she would be right *out* to get us, Agent Herring appeared through the doorway. She motioned for us to come with her.

"What can I do for you ladies?" she asked, as soon as the door closed behind us.

She led us through the police station. Her five foot eight inch frame and long legs had her a few strides ahead of us.

"We would like to talk to you about Theodore Ramirez," I said bluntly.

"What about him?" she asked.

"We know that is why you are here. We know that is the unrelated case you are investigating and we think it might be Sterling."

"What makes you think that?" Herring asked. She stopped at a desk covered with confidential FBI files.

"Well, I for one know he *was* a whack job, so I'm sure he still is. Also, if Sterling is M-I-A and this Ramirez is just an alias, it could be possible they are the same person," I suggested.

"Technically yes, it is possible. The only problem I see in your theory is that this Ramirez guy probably has a long history of arrests. Most likely he is a career criminal who started out with petty theft. Which, in turn escalated into murder," agent Herring explained.

"Maybe, but this could also be a lonely man who was afraid his girlfriend would leave, so he held her hostage for three days. He is arrested for that one and only crime. Once paroled, he assumes a new identity, holds people against their will, then to ensure they definitely won't leave, he kills them," I explained.

"How long did it take you to come up with that?" my mother asked amazed.

"Funny enough, it just came out. I was piggy backing off her suspect profile." I was hoping if I sounded like I knew what I was talking about, agent Herring would take us to the house.

"So, let's sit down, I'll take down what information you have for me and look into it," Herring said, sitting.

"Actually," I began. "We were hoping we could tag along to the crime scene and see if there was anything familiar inside."

"Look, I can't allow you to go anywhere near the house. Like you said, it is a crime scene. We will talk to the neighbors and get a description and have them come in and talk to our sketch artist. Then we will show you the mock up. I can't just volunteer information to the family of a victim."

"Please Agent Herring. I know what Sterling looks like and his mannerisms. I can help with the investigation," I pleaded.

"If you really want to help, just let us do our jobs."

"Agent, please. We want to find Gwen. I know that since this case has come up Gwendolyn's disappearance is being pushed to the back burner until this guy is caught. Even then, who's to say they would even go back to looking for her," I said.

"That is not necessarily true. We are treating her disappearance as though it is related to the case. I promise we are doing everything in our power to find her," Agent Herring said.

"Were you able to see anything from the hotel surveillance videos?" my mother asked.

"That I can tell you. There is a person of interest we have found on the video. Our technical analyst is trying to identify him so we can bring him in for questioning."

"What do you mean by person of interest? What did he do that caused suspicion?" I asked.

"He is found on the tape, as Gwendolyn is coming out of the hotel restaurant, reaching inside her purse. He retrieves something, then discards it into the same plant you said her cell phone was located when you found it."

"Anything else?"

"He is also seen going up on the elevator after her and getting off at the same floor. After that something happens to the signal and it goes to static for exactly ten minutes and the picture doesn't come back until we see you getting off the elevator on the same floor." Agent Herring averts her eyes from mine as though she doesn't want to see my reaction.

"You mean to tell me that if I hadn't sat and finished my coffee and just paid the bill, I could have caught the abduction and stopped it from happening?" Tears began to form in my eyes as I began to blame myself, yet again, for allowing Gwen to go back to the room alone.

"If he wanted her that badly, he would have found another time. This is not something you could have controlled. You were trying to help her overcome her fear of being alone in public," my mother attempted to comfort.

"No, I was trying to help her defy her mother. Doreen was the reason I even allowed it in the first place. We were talking about how stupid it was that she felt she had to ask permission to go on vacation. She is an adult and she should be able to do whatever she wanted. She was the one who suggested going up to the room alone to prove to herself and her mother that there was nothing to be afraid of." I grinded the heels of my hands into my eyes trying to erase the tears.

"So what's the next step?" my mother asked me.

"What about the media?" I asked, focusing my attention back to Agent Herring.

"We are getting together a press conference in order for you to reach out to the abductor and humanize Gwen so he may let her go. If it is Sterling again and he let her go the first time, he may let her go this time," Herring explained.

"The only problem is, Agent, he didn't let her go the first time. The police had to show up a second time with a warrant to search the property in order to find her," I explained.

"Well, he didn't physically hurt her the first time. Maybe he just plans to force her to be a part of his sick little game."

"This is not a game. It is someone's life." Herring opened her mouth to say something, but I held up my hand to stop her and continued, "I understand *he* may think it's a game, but *I* am taking this seriously."

"Herring, I think we've got something," Agent Jarvis said, poking his head out of an office ten feet away from the desk where we were sitting.

"Stay here, I'll be right back," Herring said before walking away.

I waited for the door to the office to close before rifling through the files on the desk.

"What are you doing?" my mother asked.

"Just watch the office and let me know if someone comes out of there," I told her.

I found the file on Theodore Ramirez, grabbed a piece of scrap paper that was on the desk and wrote down the address from the file. Closing the file, I folded the piece of paper and stuffed it into my pocket by the time my mother smacked me on the shoulder. I looked up and saw Herring and Jarvis emerge from the office. I had what I wanted and decided it was time to go.

"Thank you for your time, Agent Herring. I hope you are able to find Gwendolyn, alive and unharmed. Please let us know when the press conference is and I will make sure we have Doreen with us," I said, as I shook her hand.

"The press conference will be tomorrow at ten a.m. Please bring Laird and your father along as well. It will be right out front. Most likely the local police will be here to back you, but the other two agents and I have been called to the next county over for assistance. We will be in touch and let you know if we find anything," Herring said, with a confused look on her face from my change in demeanor.

My mother and I decided to go back to the hotel to catch up with the others. I figured since we had the location and knew where to go, it was eminent to get there as soon as possible.

Fourteen

When we arrived back to the hotel room, my cell phone rang. I couldn't imagine who it was considering all the people who normally call me were either in the room with me or missing.

"Hello?" I answered, putting the call on speaker.

"You're going to be next," the male caller stated.

"Excuse me?" I replied.

"I'm going to slit your throat and dispose of your body where no one will find you."

I pulled the piece of paper out of my pocket and handed it to my mother. She wrote down the number displayed on the caller ID. Everyone else in the room was silent.

"Who is this?" I asked.

"You don't recognize my voice, Anjenette?" he replied.

'If he knows my name, I have to know this person from somewhere,' I thought. I just couldn't place the voice.

"I'm sorry, I don't. Why don't you tell me who you are so we can try and resolve this issue," I spoke in a calm tone.

"Don't try to use your lawyer voice to coax me into revealing anything to you. You should know who I am and when you figure it out, you should be scared. I've been watching you, following you. I saw you at the café and I know where you're staying. Be on the lookout, I'm coming for you."

The call disconnected and I didn't know what to say. I could feel everyone's eyes on me as I stared down at the phone.

"Who was that Anjie?" Doreen asked.

"I'm not sure, but I think it was Mateo. It definitely wasn't Sterling," I revealed.

"What do we do now?" my mother asked, handing the paper back to me.

"We should call the police and report it. That man was threatening you," my father said.

"Whatever that was can wait. If we report a threatening phone call to the police now, they are going to think we are looking for attention. We need to focus on finding Gwen. Agent Herring said they were treating her disappearance as though it was related to the Ramirez case, but I have my doubts. I feel it was just a ruse to pacify my questioning. I have the address to the house where the bodies were found. If we work in teams, we can interview the neighbors who live closest to the house."

"There are only five of us and in order for the team plan to work there needs to be six. How is that going to work out?" Doreen asked.

"I think my father can hold his own. Doreen and Laird, I say you talk to the five neighbors to the left of the house. Dad, you're going to the five neighbors to the right of the house and mom and I will talk to every neighbor across the street who can see the house from their driveway. Also, Herring says the press conference is tomorrow morning at ten," I explained.

"I was hoping to have the press conference today so we could get the word out as soon as possible," Doreen complained.

"At least we are getting media attention. I'm sure more people come up missing and the only people who know they are missing are their family and the police. For now I think we should focus on the neighbor interviews."

"What if they aren't home?" Doreen asked.

"It's Sunday night. Where are they going to be?" I responded.

"It is a three day weekend. You and Gwen left for the weekend."

"Let's just check out of the hotel, go talk to the neighbors and if they aren't home, we can figure it out from there."

"We can't check out of the hotel. What about the press conference tomorrow? This is the last place Gwen was seen. I want to stay here in case she either comes back or she is found."

"We have homes to go back to and jobs. We can't live our lives hoping something happens. If we don't work, we don't get paid and eventually our money will run out and the hotel will ask us to leave. Let's go talk to the neighbors and go home. We can drive back here tomorrow for the press conference," Laird laid it all out for Doreen.

"Now you're on their side. You think Gwenie's not coming back either. I can't believe this. How could you do this to me?" Doreen acted as though we were giving up.

"We aren't doing anything *to* you. We are doing this *for* Gwendolyn," I declared.

"You keep telling yourself that. I'll stay here and wait for word from my daughter." Doreen grabbed ahold of the underside of the chair she sat on as though to clamp herself down.

"Fine, you stay here and sulk while the rest of us go out there and actually do something productive in the search for Gwendolyn." I stood and began to pack my suitcase.

"Doreen honey," Laird began. "We can't just sit around and wait for something to happen."

"Exactly, I have the information needed to get one step closer to finding Gwen and you want to sit and do nothing? Fine, you wallow in self-pity, while the rest of us actually do something productive," I said, stuffing all I had brought with me into my suitcase.

"I feel helpless. Like nothing we do will actually get us closer to finding Gwen," Doreen said with tears rolling down her cheeks.

I walked over, stood in front of her and looked down at a sad excuse for a woman. As I watched Doreen act like a victim, I placed my finger under her chin and forced her to look up at me.

She stared me in the eye as I raised my right arm, held it out as far as I could, brought it back and like a sling shot slung my arm around, making sure my hand came into contact with her face. I slapped her, hard, across the cheek. She let go of the chair and placed her hands on top of the print I had made.

The palm of my hand as well as my fingertips were tingling from the force of impact. Everyone in the room gasped. I grabbed her by the arms and forced her into a standing position in front of me.

"Now, are you ready to man up, or are you going to continue to sit here and cry like a little bitch?" I yelled in her face.

"Alright, just please don't hit me again," Doreen said, stepping over toward Laird and away from me.

"Now, help me pack up Gwen's bag so we can go," I said, bouncing the suitcase my friend brought with her onto one of the beds.

We finished packing both suitcases and checked out of the hotel. Considering we all arrived separately, we all left together, but in our separate vehicles. I had the address so they followed me.

The neighborhood Ramirez's house was located in looked like any other neighborhood. There were established homes in the front. Some needed new paint, roof shingles and siding, some had been well maintained. The newer homes were in the back. Those of which were either less than a year old or still under warranty. He apparently didn't want to stick out, so he purchased a home in the middle of the neighborhood. It appeared to be between eight and twelve years old.

It was a ranch style one story home with exquisite landscaping. Either he really cared about his home's appearance or he was just trying to hide the fact that he was killing people inside. The home itself could have used a good power washing down the driveway and along the walk way, other than that it was in good shape.

The house was surrounded by police tape. It was strung up between two trees and attached to the house to block off the entry way. Uniformed officers were standing around the outside of the perimeter to regulate the people entering the crime scene. There were a couple of police cars parked at the curb, most likely to keep away the looters and snoopers.

We all gathered around in front of my car and I handed out steno note pads. One to my father, one to Laird and one for my mother and me.

"Everyone has their assignments and the basic questions to ask. Don't give away any information, we want *them* to tell *us* who he is," I told them.

I used the same tactics on my clients. It was how I could tell whether or not I was prosecuting an innocent victim or a heartless bastard.

We all decided to start furthest from the house, then work our way back to the cars, which were parked along the curb across the street from the house of horrors.

The first house my mother and I went to was a powder blue two story. I'm sure that if Ramirez buried anything in his garden, this neighbor would have seen him do it. Of course it had nothing to do with the fact that the upstairs front room had two different windows that overlooked perfectly in the direction of the house and everything to do with the nosey old lady who had been watching us from that room since we had arrived.

I stepped up to the front door and pressed the doorbell. My mother watched from the driveway to see if the old lady left the window to answer the door.

A young man, probably her son, opened the front door. He was a very handsome, suave looking man. He wore jeans and a deep blue polo shirt, which had been well pressed. The top three buttons were open and showed off his well-built chest. His brown hair was groomed in a way that suggested possible military background.

"Can I help you?" he asked.

"My name is Anjenette and this is Carrie Anne. My best friend Gwendolyn is missing and we have reason to believe your neighbor Theodore Ramirez is behind her disappearance. Would you be willing to answer a few questions for us?" I began, trying to swallow my urge to shout out how good looking he was.

"Sure, come on in." He stepped aside allowing us access to his well decorated home.

We followed him to the living room and sat on the sofa. We declined the offer of a drink and I flipped the cover open to the steno notebook to take notes.

"Can you give me a physical description of Theodore Ramirez?" I began.

"First of all, we all called him Ted. He had dark hair with sharp facial features. His eyes were green and he was very athletic. We went running together every morning."

The fact that he went running every morning explained his toned body. I had to try really hard to listen to his words. I was imagining what his body would feel like if I rubbed my hands down his chest.

"Is there anything you can tell us about his personality?" my mother asked, when she realized I was day dreaming.

"Well, he was a great guy. Everyone around here liked him. He would though get really angry if anyone asked about his house or his history."

"What do you mean by really angry?" I asked.

"There was one time in particular where we had just finished our run and I made it a point to stop in front of his house. It was ninety six degrees outside with a heat index of a hundred and five and we were both sweating profusely. I asked if I could go inside and grab me a bottle of water. It was almost as if a switch in his brain had flipped. He immediately began screaming at me. He was telling me how water isn't free and being that we live in a well to do neighborhood, I should be able to afford my own water."

"What did you say?" my mother asked, as if we were gossiping.

"I didn't know what to say. He took off into his house and I could hear the dead bolt slide into place. I stood there for a moment. I was befuddled by his reaction."

"Could you hear anything going on in his house? Like was he talking to anyone?" I asked.

"No one ever heard anything going on in his house. It was almost as if he had the whole place sound proof so we couldn't hear him," he answered.

"Was he social with the rest of the neighborhood?" I questioned.

"In that aspect, he pretty much kept to himself. Others in the neighborhood would invite him to parties and things of that nature, but he always refused, saying he had to work or his dog was sick – even though no one ever saw a dog."

"Did he have any distinguishing marks? Any strange characteristics? His walk or scars, tattoos?"

"No tattoos that anyone saw, but he did have a few scars on his arms. He said as a child his older brother would beat on him and that was where they came from, but if you ask me, which you are, they looked like scratches from someone attempting to defend themselves from him."

"That would make sense considering he was kidnapping people to taxidermy. Did you ever suspect there was anything going on in his house?" I asked.

"I thought he was maybe a crazy porn addict and maybe it was all over his house, or something, but I never suspected he was killing anyone. Now that I think about it, there was one time he brought home a girl and I was outside. He picked her up out of the car and carried her inside. I figured because of the late hour she was drunk," he answered.

"Is there anything significant about that moment that you can think of why it seemed strange?"

"Well, the next morning around seven, he was on the driveway washing and detailing his car."

"People do that all the time," my mother commented.

"Yes, but not while wearing rubber gloves," he said, pulling his right foot up and resting it on his left knee and leaning back into the chair he occupied.

"What kind of rubber gloves?" I inquired.

"The kind you would wear if you were performing surgery."

"Tell me about the clothes he wore. Was there anything strange about his clothes?"

"He had his own sense of style. Don't get me wrong, what he wore, he wore it well. It just didn't go together."

"What do you mean?"

"When one half of your body looks like you're going to the beach and the other half looks like you're teaching a college course, it is hard to figure a person out," he said, shrugging.

"I know what you mean. It is difficult to understand a person with conflicting ideals," I said, smiling.

"That is true," he said, with a sweet smile on his face.

Our eyes locked and for several moments we stared at each other, smiling. I could feel the connection between the two of us. I realized the longing stare was causing my mother to become uncomfortable when she nudged my leg with her knee.

"Well, thank you for your time. I'm sorry, what did you say your name was?" I asked, extending my hand.

"Tony. Tony Voss," he replied, shaking my hand.

"Mr. Voss, I really appreciate your time. If you think of anything else you would like to share, or if you just want to talk, please feel free to call me," I said, handing him my card.

"Oh, you're a lawyer? Me too. I think I will call you sometime, but it won't be to talk about Ted." His smile lit up his whole face and I giggled like a high school girl who had a crush on her teacher.

"Thank you for your time," my mother said, ushering me out of Tony's house.

"He was cute," I said, once we had made it to the neighbor's driveway.

"Let's just finish talking to these neighbors without you getting another date. I thought we were here to talk about Sterling?" my mother said as she walked up the driveway to the front door of the next house.

I turned to look back at Tony's house. I could see the elderly woman still standing in the upstairs window.

Fifteen

Later that evening we all met back at the home Gwen and I shared. Every one of his neighbors said the same thing about him. He was a nice guy, just a little weird if anyone asked about his house or his past.

"No one suspected him as a killer. Everyone seemed to like him," I said.

"Apparently. The neighbors we talked to said they invited him to every party they ever had, but he always had an excuse to get out of it," Doreen added.

"If he wanted friends so badly he felt as though he had to preserve them in his house, why didn't he just look around his neighborhood? They all wanted to be friends with him," I pondered.

"Maybe it wasn't the fact that he wanted friends. Maybe he just wanted a family. He didn't want to be alone. The neighbors all had their own houses to go home to. The people in his house would never leave. He would never have to say good bye to them," my mother pointed out.

"That is true. Maybe he didn't want to form personal relationships with real people because they always leave. His mother left when he was in his adolescents and his father died when he was in his teens. His aunt and uncle never had a real relationship with him and once a month would come and go leaving him in the house alone," I informed.

"The only problem is that not everyone whose parents leave or die when they are young turn out to be serial killers. He had to have already been unstable before that and his parents' departure had to have triggered something in his mind," my father chimed in.

"Exactly, something set him off in order for him to start killing. I do agree with Agent Herring though. If he didn't physically harm Gwen the first time, there might be something about her that makes him want to keep her alive. Maybe he thinks he can convince her to love him so she will stay of her own free will," I said.

"In the morning we can take the info that we have to the FBI and tell them who Sterling was and notify them we are sure he is Theodore Ramirez," my mother said.

"Why don't we go through some pictures from high school so we can show them to the FBI? That way they can have a head start as to who they are looking for," Doreen suggested.

"Great idea. Also, don't they have some kind of software where they age enhance him to make him look older?"

I was surprised to see Doreen and my mother getting along. They never liked each other before and I am sure never had an actual conversation that didn't include screaming insults at one another. I was glad to see them getting along and hoped that this tragedy would bring us all together.

"Of course, the age enhancement software. Brilliant! The pictures we provide them with could be uploaded and digitally enhanced so they can see what he looks like today and they can take those photos to the neighbors to see if they identify him as the same person," I said.

"So how do we explain the neighbor interviews? Agent Herring didn't exactly offer the information to us. You stole the address from a file off her desk," my mother informed me.

"We don't even have to mention it. All we have to do is take the pictures in and ask the FBI to use them. We don't have to tell them we even spoke to the neighbors."

"I thought that was the whole point of talking to the neighbors," Doreen mentioned.

"No, the point of talking to the neighbors was to confirm we are following a promising lead," I told her.

"That makes sense. We don't want to be chasing someone who turns out to be just another psycho," my mother said.

I pulled out a photo box with every picture I had taken throughout middle and high school. We went through all the photographs and separated the ones I had from when Gwen and I were in high school and she was dating Sterling. We even cut out his senior photo from the yearbook.

"Okay, this pile looks good. I think we have enough," Laird commented, as we picked up any photos that didn't include Sterling.

"Yeah, we should get going it has been a long day," my mother said, as everyone stood from the table.

"We can just pick up where we left off in the morning," I said as I gathered all the photos and neighbor interviews and slipped them into a file folder.

"We are going to need to get an early start if we are going to make it to the press conference," Doreen said.

"Let's meet back here at six thirty so we can leave by seven. That should give us enough time to make it there, hand over the photos to Agent Herring and prepare to speak to the press," I said.

We said our good byes and everyone headed toward the front of the house. I walked them to the door and watched as each of them piled into the vehicles they came in. As soon as they had backed out of the driveway, I closed and bolted the front door. I headed upstairs to my bedroom for the night. I didn't really have the energy to shower, so I decided I would do that in the morning.

I changed into my night clothes and climbed into bed. I was practically asleep before my head hit the pillow.

A few hours later, I was awoken by the feeling of being watched. I rolled over slowly to look at the clock on my bed side table. Three forty two. Shifting onto my back I scanned the room for anything that seemed out of place. A dark figure stood in the corner across the room. I kept my eyes locked on the figure. My entire body was tingling.

I knew I still had a few more hours before the sun would come up and was hoping the person in the corner couldn't tell I was awake. I continued to surveill the room until having to get up to go to the bathroom and convince myself to budge.

Sitting up on the bed, I dangled my legs over the side and slid myself into a standing position. I practically floated through the room to the lavatory door, which was only four feet from the dark figure, holding my breath the whole time. My entire body trembled as I passed through the door frame.

I exhaled quietly, realizing I was vulnerable at that point and hoped the person waited until I was done before doing anything to me. When I had finished and redressed myself, I took a couple of deep breaths. I had to get out of the house.

I emerged from the bathroom, leaving the light on, and scanned the bedroom. The person who was in the corner was now standing next to my bed staring at me. I could see his face.

"Mateo, what are you doing here?" I asked him.

"I told you I was going to slit your throat," he responded with a calm tone.

"Get out of my house before I call the cops." I was hoping he couldn't hear the wavering tone in my voice.

"They won't make it in time," he said, as he produced a switchblade from the pocket of his pants.

"So you were the one who called me?"

"I can't believe you didn't figure that out sooner," he said. His tone at that point was angry.

"I don't have time to play your games. I am trying to find my friend who has been missing for two days."

"This is no game Anjenette. You have brushed me off for too long and now you're going to pay."

He lunged forward at me. I darted toward my only way out and pulled the bedroom door open. The whole house was dark, but I had lived there long enough to know my way around. I ran down the stairs to the front door. It was bolted and the switch to unlock it was broken off.

I heard him at the top of the stairs, so I headed for the back door. He had broken that one as well. I was locked in my own house with a man who wanted to kill me. I didn't have time to find the perfect hiding place so I reached for a kitchen knife. The only problem was the butcher block was empty. I ducked behind the counter, unarmed.

'How long had he been in the house?' I wondered.

"Anjenette, you can't hide from me," he said in a sing song way.

As I listened for the sound of his footsteps, I could hear him in the living room. I had to make my way back up the stairs to my bedroom for my phone. It had been left charging on my nightstand.

Crawling along the floor and down the hallway, I passed the living room without him noticing me. I quietly made my way up the stairs and into my bedroom. The bathroom light was still illuminated. Closing the door, I engaged the lock. There was so much adrenalin running through my body, I was able to push my dresser along the carpet to barricade myself in.

Grabbing my phone, charger and all, I took it into the bathroom with me. I closed and locked that door as well. His footsteps were heavy on the stairs as he made his way back up.

I pressed the button on the side of my phone to irradiate the screen. He was banging on the bedroom door at that point. Swiping my finger along the screen, I attempted to unlock it. My hands were shaking and the first few times I got the code wrong.

"Stupid smartphone," I yelled at the device wringing it with my hands.

"Anjie, you can't stop me," he shouted, still banging on the door.

I took a couple of deep breaths and swiped the unlock code again. It worked and my home screen appeared. Luckily, the dresser was holding him off long enough for me to access the phone feature on my device. Touching the icon for phone, selecting keypad, I dialed nine-one-one.

'I am going to get a regular cell phone that only makes phone calls when I get out of this,' I thought to myself.

"Nine-one-one, what is your emergency?" the operator came on the line quickly.

"A man has broken into my house and is threatening to kill me. He has a knife," I told her.

"Okay ma'am, where is the intruder right now?"

"He is outside my bedroom door. I barricaded it with my dresser and locked myself in my bathroom."

BANG, BANG, BANG! It sounded as though he was putting all his weight into the door.

"Is that him banging on the door?" the emergency operator asked.

"Yes, please hurry. He broke the locks on the two main entrance doors to my house so I am locked in."

She verified my name and address with me and assured me a patrol car was on the way. "Please stay on the line with me until the police arrive."

"Okay, but please hurry."

Mateo continued to bang on the bedroom door. I was sitting in the middle of the bathroom floor, hugging my knees and holding the phone to my ear.

"Are you still there?" the emergency operator asked.

"Yes." It came out more as a breath.

"He is almost there. Can you hear the siren?"

"Yes, I can hear it. Thank you so much," I said before disconnecting the call.

Regardless of the fact that the police came down the street with sirens blaring, Mateo continued to bang on the bedroom door. I heard the front door bust open and the banging on my bedroom door stopped. I unlocked the bathroom door and opened it enough to poke my head out. The dresser hadn't budged.

"Sheriff's department. Get on the ground. Drop your weapon and get on the ground!" I heard a voice yell from the top of the stairs.

I heard one more loud bang on the door just before I heard someone knock. I assumed it was the officer slamming Mateo into the door to handcuff him.

"Ms. Marcum? This is the police. Are you okay in there?" a man's voice asked.

I emerged from my bunker. Most of my adrenaline had drained once the police showed up, so I was having trouble moving the dresser away from the door.

"Yeah, I'm okay," I said through the closed door.

"Can you open the door for me?" the officer asked.

"Is he still out there?"

"No ma'am, he is outside in the patrol car with my partner."

I used all my strength to move the dresser just far enough away from the door so I could get it open. On the other side of the threshold stood a uniformed officer.

"Is anyone else in the house?" he asked.

"No, just me," I said stepping out of the room.

We headed downstairs toward the kitchen. I wanted to illuminate the entire house, so I flipped on every light switch we passed. I knew there was no way I was going to sleep now, so I started a pot of coffee.

"Ms. Marcum, is there someone you can call to come over? Both dead bolts for your exterior doors are going to need to be replaced and we busted your front door open. Your home is no longer secure," the officer informed me.

"I could call my parents," I said.

"Good, now if you offer me some of that coffee you're brewing, I will gladly stay with you until they arrive."

"Oh, of course, thank you. I don't think I could be alone right now."

"I understand," the officer said, as he sat down at my kitchen table.

I had my cell phone clutched in my hand all the way from the bathroom to the kitchen. Turning it in my hands, I stared at it before dialing my parents. My father answered the phone with a scruffy voice suggesting I had woken him up.

"Anjie? What's wrong?" he asked, without even saying 'hello' first.

"Daddy, can you and Mom come over right now?" I said, tears burning my eyes.

"Is everything okay?" he asked.

"I just need y'all to come over. I will tell you what happened when you get here," I said before disconnecting the call, so he couldn't ask any more questions. I turned toward the officer. "They should be on their way."

"What are you going to do about your doors?" the officer asked.

"There isn't really anything I *can* do until the hardware stores open," I informed him.

"That's true. While we wait, do you mind if I ask you some questions?"

"It would make the time go by faster rather than sitting here in silence," I suggested, rubbing the tears from my eyes before they escaped.

"Do you happen to know why this man broke into your house?" the officer asked.

"He is a rapist I prosecuted a while back. He also beat my client into submission. He had suggested a few times that he wanted to kill me, but I thought he was harmless. A few weeks ago he cornered me in the parking garage of my office and pulled out a gun. He only shot at the light above my car."

"Did you report this incident?"

"No, I just figured it was an isolated incident. I never expected him to break into my house. Besides, the security officer in the garage had called someone; I assumed it was the police."

"I will check into that and see if it was reported. If we have that on file as well, this gentleman could go to jail for a while."

The officer's words weren't exactly encouraging.

Once my parents arrived, the officer left. After starting another pot of coffee to brew, I sat down at the table with them, and told them what happened with Mateo. By the time I had finished my recollection of events, the sun was beginning to peek out. My father decided he would go to the hardware store for the deadbolts as I headed back upstairs to shower. Every light was on in the house and I wasn't planning to turn them off until the sun made its full appearance.

My shower was longer than normal, using that time to think about my interactions with Mateo. I knew there was no reason to try and rationalize the mind of a criminal, but I couldn't figure out why of all the women he had come in contact with, why he had chosen me?

Turning the faucet knob to the right, in order to turn off the water, I reached up and pulled the terrycloth rectangle down from the white plastic bar in my shower and wrapped myself in the towel. Pulling back the curtain, stepping out onto the shag bath mat, I stood in front of the mirror for a few moments glaring at my reflection. Due to my lack of sleep over the past couple of nights, dark circles had formed under my eyes. I pulled out my make-up bag from under the sink and set it on the counter.

Walking over to my dresser, I opened the top drawer and chose my undergarments. After what I had just experienced, I pushed aside all the matching sets and lacy panties and chose the beige control top along with a plain white sports bra. The next drawer down was pants. Jeans were classic and still made me feel feminine with a hint of roughness.

Dropping the towel, I dressed in the items I had so far, then headed over to my closet for a shirt. As I examined the contents, I noticed an unconscious pattern I had developed. I never realized it before, but all my clothing hanging in my closet was color coded. With the bright colors in the front and the dark colors further toward the back just in front of my dresses, which were hung by length. Since black was the color of choice when someone loses a loved one, I pulled on a plain black tee and tucked it into the waist of my pants.

Back to the bathroom, I stood in front of the mirror analyzing my hair. As I watched my reflection pull the brush from scalp to end, I remembered a time when Gwen and I had first moved into that house and we shared the master bedroom. She said it was because she was scared that someone would break into the house and take me away from her, but I knew it was because she didn't want to be alone. I let her share the room with me anyway. It was like having a sleep over every night.

After a year had passed, she had decided she needed her own room, so she moved all her stuff into the room across the hall. Every Monday, though, she would come into my room when I was getting ready for work and she would brush my hair while I did my make-up. It always saved me an extra twenty minutes. She would only do that on Mondays and I could never figure out what was so special about that day. I decided that when we found her, I was going to ask. It was Monday and as odd as I thought it was before, I had missed our morning together.

After plastering my face with make-up to hide my fatigue, I headed back downstairs and found Gwen's parents had arrived and they, along with my mother, were huddled around my breakfast table. They appeared to be looking over what pictures and information we had.

"Good morning," I announced as I entered the room. "When did y'all get here?"

"About an hour ago. We discussed this last night. We were supposed to be here early since it is a two hour drive out to the police station and we have a press conference in two and a half hours," Doreen said.

"Have I been upstairs that long?" I said, realizing my father had finished changing the deadbolt on the front door and was now in the process of finishing with the one on the back door.

"You have been up there for a long time," my mother informed.

"Well, okay then. I guess we should get going," I said, joining them at the table.

"As soon as your father is finished securing your house, we can be out the door," my mother commented.

"Does anyone have an actual plan as to what we are going to tell the police and FBI agents about how we acquired the address to the Ramirez home as well as why we spoke to his neighbors?" I asked.

"We could always just say we Googled it," Doreen said. "We can figure out the rest of the details on the way, let's go."

My mother compiled all the information into a file folder as Doreen and Laird stood up. My father finished with the dead bolt and I headed toward the coffee maker to refill my cup when Doreen stopped me.

"What are you doing?" She asked.

"What does it look like I'm doing?" I responded.

"There is no time for that. We need to go now while it is still early. I do not want to get stuck in traffic," she said, grabbing my arm.

"You better make time for it. I didn't get much sleep last night and I need more coffee. Arguing about it is only going to take longer. Now let me fill my cup and we can go," I told her, yanking my arm from her grasp.

I filled a travel mug and poured in a little creamer while Doreen fidgeted by the front door. I had to grab my shoes as I was shuffled through the door in a rush to leave.

Sixteen

As we approached the front doors to the police station, Officer Samuels and FBI Agent Jarvis were headed out.

"Mr. and Mrs. Welsh, Mr. and Mrs. Marcum, Anjenette. To what do I owe the pleasure?" Samuels greeted us.

"We have some information that may be able to conclude that Sterling Bigum is the one who was living in the home registered under the name Theodore Ramirez," my mother told them, handing over the file with all the information we had gathered.

"Thank you for the information. We will look it over and if we find out anything about Gwendolyn, we will let you know," Agent Jarvis dismissed us.

"You can't just turn us away," I said aggressively. As he turned to continue to leave, I grabbed his arm.

"This is not your investigation," Jarvis said, pulling his arm from my grasp and stepping up to me. "If you continue to get in the way, I will have you arrested for the obstruction of justice."

"We are trying to help. In no way are we obstructing justice. I tell you this much, we will not stop until we find Gwendolyn, with or without your help." I turned to walk away.

"We are trying to help you find our daughter. If you decide not to accept it, that's fine, but at least hear us out. We actually have some information that could be useful to you," Doreen said, through clenched teeth.

After several moments of silence, Jarvis conceded. "Alright, let's go inside and talk. I'm sure Agent Herring would be interested. You can discuss it with her. Samuels and I were just on our way out."

We were lead through the police station into an office with a large mahogany desk positioned almost in the center of the room. There were several bookshelves containing law and psychology manuals, along the wall behind the desk. A brown leather sofa was set up in one corner of the room facing the desk with a coffee table approximately two feet in front of it.

Jarvis left us there without saying a word. Only a few moments had passed before Agent Herring entered the room, looking very displeased and holding the file we had passed to Jarvis. The five of us attempted to fit on the sofa together except my father and Laird ended up on the arms of the couch on opposite ends and I sat in the middle between my mother and Doreen.

Agent Herring moved the desk chair out from behind the desk and stopped it on the other side of the table. She sat down and slammed the file folder onto the table.

"I have briefly looked over the materials you brought. How did you get the address to the house in order to obtain the neighbor interviews?" she asked, sounding furious.

"I peeked at the files on the desk when my mother and I came in to talk to you," I confessed.

"I can't believe you! I specifically told you to let us do our jobs and we would handle the investigation," she scolded.

"I'm sorry, but we can't just sit around and hope you find Gwendolyn. We need to feel proactive," I said.

"It has only been a couple of days and we are still gathering evidence. What more can I do to get you to stay out of the investigation?" Herring asked.

"I don't want to receive a phone call one day telling me you found my daughter's body. I want to help in the rescue of my daughter and find her alive," Doreen added.

"I understand your concern, but that is what we are here for. It is our job to conduct neighbor interviews, which we have," Herring said.

"We know it is your job, but we are able to ask questions you may not have thought to ask. We also brought photos of Sterling you could use in your age enhancing program to ask the neighbors if that is Theodore Ramirez," I pointed out.

"We have his mug shot from when he was arrested to do that with."

"The photos we brought are a little less intimidating."

"Sterling Bigum has gone MIA and according to his parole officer he hasn't checked in for months. Everything with the name Theodore Ramirez has now been shut down. Credit cards, bank accounts, vehicles, everything except that house has been closed or sold. Now, I understand you want to help, so please tell me everything you remember about him so we can nail this guy," Herring requested.

We went over everything we could remember about him from high school. I had a few more memories than the rest, but we all had helpful information.

"What can you tell me about the clothes he wore? Was there anything unusual about the way he dressed?" Herring asked.

"It wasn't unusual about what he wore; it was more about how he wore it," I said.

"What does that mean?"

"Some days he would dress in jeans and a dress shirt with a tie and others he would wear dress pants and a tank top. One day he came to school in what we thought were swim trunks and a tweed jacket. He wore a tie with it, no shirt and flip flops. It was almost as if he was trying to start a trend that no one wanted to catch on to."

"Maybe it's called indivisually," a female voice said in the doorway.

We all turned to look and saw a woman, who looked older than her time, with long brown hair standing just inside the room. She was using the door frame to hold herself up. I recognized her as Sterling's aunt and she appeared to be three sheets to the wind. Her eyes were red rimmed and I couldn't tell if that was from the alcohol or if she had been crying.

"Mrs. Bigum?" I said as I stood and walked toward her.

"Sterling's mother? I thought she died?" Doreen blurted.

"No, his father died. His mother just left town," my mother informed.

"I'm his aunt, you damn floozy. These peopo called me here 'cause you won't leab my nephew alone. Tryin' dasay dat sweet boy kidnap Gwen again. Dat only haben one time 'cause da poor boy was lonely." Her words were slurred and she swayed as she talked.

"Mrs. Bigum, where is Sterling now?" Agent Herring asked.

"Dunno. Changed his name ta get away from bein' called a kidnabber and left. Last time I hear from him he wuz in Europe."

Her words sounded more like she was uneducated than drunk, but I figured alcohol made people stupid anyway. I stood next to her just in case she fell over.

"What about your husband? Do you know if he has heard from Sterling?" Herring asked her.

Mrs. Bigum's eyes glazed over and she rolled back on her heels as if she was going to pass out right there. I placed one hand on the middle of her back and grabbed her arm to try to stabilize her. She blinked her eyes quickly as though she were remembering where she was. She looked over at me and scowled.

"Getcher hands off me," she said, yanking her arm away from my grasp.

"Are you drunk?" I asked her, quietly.

"I'mma grow up. I can drink if I wanna."

"I think we should continue this interview some other time when you're feeling better. Do you need a ride home?"

"I'm fine. Eder we do dis now or notatal. I done eber wanna see deez peopo 'gain."

"That is understandable. How about you wait in the office next door and I will be right with you," Herring told her.

I returned to my seat on the sofa as Herring assisted Sterling's aunt to the next room over.

"Well, that was interesting. I hope she didn't start drinking because we accused Sterling of those murders and Gwen's abduction," I said, as Agent Herring returned.

"She has to realize that as of right now all the evidence points to Sterling. He has kidnapped Gwen before and now he is missing as well. The only way this could turn around is if we found *his* body," she announced.

"Wouldn't that be something? If that were to happen we would be out of ideas," Doreen said.

"Don't worry Mrs. Welsh, I'm sure if we showed the neighbors Sterling's picture, they would identify him as Theodore Ramirez."

"How can you guarantee that? We only say we are sure it is him because we want to believe it. It makes it easier for us to already have a suspect in mind and already have him persecuted," I explained. "Also, if you watch her latest vlog posting, Sterling is coaching her in the background."

"That is how our legal system works. Pick the most convenient suspect and go after him," Herring said, as she gathered a couple of files off the desk.

"Oh, I know how the legal system works. I'm a prosecutor," I told her laughing.

"Now that makes sense," Herring snickered. "I'm going to talk with Mrs. Bigum. If I find out anything else, I'll contact you. The press conference is going to be set up out front. Agent Fleck is out there waiting for you."

"Thank you Agent Herring," Doreen said.

"No problem, Mrs. Welsh. It is my job to make sure we find your daughter. We are all hoping it is soon and she is unharmed."

Herring left the office. As the five of us walked through the station, we passed the room where Sterling's aunt was waiting for the agent. She had laid down on the sofa, in the fetal position, and passed out. We continued on, headed out to the press conference.

Fleck was standing in front of the station where a podium had been set up. Camera crews and reporters began filming and snapping pictures as we emerged. The agent approached us and handed Doreen a framed eight by ten photo of Gwendolyn.

"If you have a framed photo, it tends to give her meaning and more people feel sympathetic to your situation. All you have to do is stand up at the podium and explain who she is and what happened to her. Plead to the man who took her to bring her back. Let them know she is loved and missed," Fleck told them.

Doreen nodded and began to cry. Laird's eyes became blood-shot and red rimmed. No tears formed, but he appeared as though he had been crying.

They stepped up to the podium while my parents and I stayed back. Fleck handed the Welsh's a few note cards with certain things they should talk about.

"This is our daughter, Gwendolyn Welsh," Doreen said, showing the photo to the cameras. "She has been missing since Saturday morning. If anyone has any information as to her whereabouts please contact the Sundaisy police department. To the man who has taken her, we miss her and want her back. Please let her go so she can come home to us."

She turned her head and produced a tissue from her pocket in which she used to blow her nose. I was hoping the news stations would edit that part out. Agent Fleck nudged Doreen and turned her focus to the note cards. She shuffled through the three by five white cards, then turned back toward the podium.

"She is five feet six inches tall and has shoulder length brown hair. She was last seen wearing blue jeans and a purple sweat shirt at the Rizzy Hotel and Spa. She likes...uhh...she uhh..." Doreen couldn't finish. She looked down at the cards in her hand and shook her head. "I'm sorry. I'm supposed to tell you her hobbies and things she likes to do. I think those things are completely irrelevant to the fact that my baby girl, my only child is missing and there is a psycho out there who has her. Please, somebody knows something. Just contact the police and give them as much information as possible so our daughter can be rescued.

Seventeen

After they talked to the press, we drove away from the police station. We had decided to go to the Ramirez house of horrors. Since the bodies had been removed and we were sure they had collected all the evidence they needed, we thought we might be able to wander the house. Just out of curiosity, we wanted to see how he lived.

We pulled up to the curb, across the street from the crime scene. There were crime scene investigators and the coroner along with Officer Samuels and FBI Agent Jarvis. At first we watched as black plastic body bags were being carried from the backyard and piled into the coroner's van. The back doors were open, exposing a mound of covered dead bodies.

"There wasn't anyone here yesterday when we stopped by to talk to the neighbors," Laird pointed out.

"They must have found more bodies out back," Doreen said, stating the obvious.

"He must have buried the bodies that didn't preserve well," I assumed.

After a few moments, Agent Herring pulled up accompanied by Agent Fleck. The five of us exited the vehicle and headed over to where Samuels and Jarvis were standing.

"Now what is going on? I thought all the bodies were removed," I said, glaring at Samuels.

"This is still an ongoing investigation. You people need to go home and allow us to do our job," Samuels said, stretching his arms out to his sides as though he was trying to hold us back.

"My daughter is missing and instead of you trying to find her, you are standing around a house talking about a crime that is now over. My daughter's crime still exists and nothing is being done to find her," Doreen ranted.

"As you can clearly see, this is far from over. On top of that, we *are* trying to find her Mrs. Welsh. We are looking for clues here to see if maybe she was here at any point in time," Samuels said, with an uncaring tone in his voice.

"I thought I told you to go home and let us take care of this," Herring said, as she and Fleck stepped up to the group of us.

"I just told them that, Herring," Samuels said.

"This is not taking care of it. This is dwelling on the past. Please, go find my daughter," Doreen screamed.

"Where do we look? We have no leads and we can't wander the city aimlessly hoping to spot her walking down the street. We *are* trying to find her," Jarvis said.

"Didn't he leave evidence of something that someone at your labs can identify so you know where he has been and where he would take her?" Doreen said.

"You watch too much T.V. The fact that on television they can get DNA and trace samples within minutes, real life doesn't work that way. Some of the evidence we find can take weeks or even months to get the results. Not only that, but there is no way to guess as to where he might have taken her," Samuels declared.

"Agents, I think you should see this," a gentleman, wearing a black jacket with the words *Crime Scene Unit* printed on the back, said.

Jarvis, Fleck and Herring began making their way to the backyard. Our group started to follow, but Samuels stopped us.

"Where do you think you're going?" he asked.

"I need to know if that has something to do with my daughter," Doreen said with tears streaming down her face.

"You need to go home. We will let you know when and if we find something."

"I'm not going to sit around and hope that you keep me up to date with the investigation. This may not even have anything to do with Gwen's disappearance. In which case you are going to put her on the back burner until this case is solved. I can't wait around, hoping to hear good news. I am going to continue looking for her and I will never stop until I find out what happened to my baby girl."

"Mrs. Welch," Agent Herring said, as she emerged from the backyard and walked toward us. "If you could meet us back at the station, I have some other questions for you."

"Tell me now. What did you find?" Doreen insisted.

"Meet us back at the station and I can tell you there."

"You can tell me now."

Herring took a deep breath realizing defeat. "There was a purse buried in the yard back here with Gwendolyn's ID in the wallet. The officers are going to bag it and process it and have it sent back to the station. Once it arrives, we can allow you to take a look at it to verify it belonged to her."

Doreen fell to her knees, crying hysterically. "Not my baby. This can't be happening. Lord, please tell me my little girl is okay," she shouted, looking up to the sky.

"Come on honey. Let's head over to the station and wait so we can find out more information," Laird said, helping Doreen to her feet.

"No, I want to see it now," she shouted.

"I'm sorry ma'am, but until it has been processed, we can't allow you to see it," agent Herring said.

We headed back to the car and piled in. Laird had to practically drag Doreen over and assist her into the back seat. She cried quietly, staring out the window, while the rest of us watched the police presence multiply. Several uniformed officers appeared as though they had been chosen to transport empty body bags as they retrieved them from the trunks of their cars and carried them to the backyard. I decided we didn't need to see them come back with a full body bag, so I started the car and took off for the police station.

When we arrived, we were escorted to the same office we had been in previously. Herring had called to inform the officer at the front we were on our way so when we arrived we were immediately taken to the room and there were enough seats for everyone.

"Gwen's purse was left in the hotel room. She didn't have one on her when she was abducted," I said, as soon as we sat down.

"Then where did the purse come from?" Doreen asked.

"I don't know. Maybe it belonged to one of the other victims," I replied, shrugging.

"Then why was Gwen's ID found in it?" she inquired.

"Maybe he is using it to taunt us. I don't know. Maybe if I thought like a psychopath I could have more answers for you, but I don't," I said, feeling frustrated.

"We will find out when the agent arrives with it. Let's just sit here quietly and wait," my mother suggested.

"Oh sure, why don't we all just sit here quietly and not talk about Gwen at all? Maybe we should just forget about her all together. She's gone anyway, no reason to think about her anymore," Doreen said, practically screaming at my mother, tears streaming down her face.

"That is not what I meant and you know it. Why is it whenever you don't get your way, you decide to throw a temper tantrum like a toddler? Calm down before they come in here and arrest us for disturbing the peace," my mother scolded.

"Where is my peace?" Doreen shouted.

"Shut up, Doreen. You should really stop acting like the victim."

"How about you both shut up and we can sit here, silently reflecting," I said, taking deep cleansing breaths.

"What are we reflecting about?" Doreen asked.

"Whatever you feel is necessary for your life. If it helps you can also pray for Gwen's safe return. I have prayed every day to have my friend back," I told them, with a calm tone.

Finally everyone was quiet.

It was a little over five hours before Agent Herring and Agent Fleck joined us. It had felt like the longest five hours of my life.

Herring was carrying a paper bag sealed with red tape stating it was evidence.

She placed the bag down on the table in front of Doreen. She whispered something to Fleck and he left the room, closing the door behind him. Herring pulled the desk chair around to where it was before and sat across the table.

Doreen leaned forward and placed her hands on the bag. She closed her eyes for a few moments as though she were saying a prayer. Slipping her finger under the tape, she started to break the seal. Herring stopped her.

"The seal has to be broken by law enforcement," Herring told her, removing the bag from Doreen's grasp.

Herring turned the bag around so the seal was facing her. Using a small knife she had in her pocket, Herring cut the tape holding the bag closed. She lifted the flap and stood. A tan hand bag, which was sealed in a clear zippered plastic bag, was removed and placed on the table. I couldn't remember ever seeing it before, but Doreen's eyes welled up with tears and she placed one hand over her mouth. It was a gesture that had suggested *she* had seen it before.

"Do you recognize this, Mrs. Welch?" agent Herring asked.

Doreen nodded as she drew the handbag to her chest. "It's the purse she used to take to church every Sunday when she was growing up. Just before Sterling held her hostage, it went missing. She was always so well organized. It was odd for her not to be able to find something. At the time we didn't think anything of it. Now I'm sure this Theodore Ramirez is Sterling Bigum." Doreen leaned into Laird and he hugged her while she hugged the bag.

"You're positive it's the same one?" Herring asked.

"Absolutely," Doreen said aloud and Laird quietly nodded his head.

"I need to present a criminal profile of Sterling to the police to aid them in his capture. Anjenette, would you be willing to assist me? You know more about him anyway. Have you ever been involved in a criminal profile before?" Herring questioned.

"I was once, but I just sat in the room and listened. I have never actually said anything," I told her.

"All I will need you to do is confirm what I say. If you think of any of his mannerisms I am missing or that need to be mentioned, please feel free to jump in," she told me.

Herring and I stood, walked toward the door.

"What about Gwendolyn. They need to know who she is. I can go and tell them about her," Doreen said.

"We are only going to talk about Sterling. He is the one they need to capture. Once he is arrested, then we can go in and rescue your daughter. First things first and finding the criminal mastermind is first," Herring told her.

"So, you mean to tell me you aren't even going to mention her?" Doreen was screaming again.

"Mrs. Welsh, please lower your voice. There will be a mention of a possible surviving victim. If they are able to find the house Sterling is in now, they will know to be cautious," Herring informed.

Herring placed her hand on my lower back and began pushing me toward the exit. I assumed her new found urgency to leave was in order to discontinue the argument with Doreen.

When we arrived, the officers were piling into their meeting room. Some were sitting, others were standing. The police chief was standing in the back of the room by the door as though he were waiting to leave. Every officer pulled out a small two inch by four inch notebook and pen to write down what Agent Herring had to say.

"Thank you for being here today. I'm Agent Herring with the FBI and this is Anjenette Marcum. Her friend was abducted from The Rizzy Hotel by a man we believe to be the abductee's ex-boyfriend.

"The man we are looking for is Sterling Bigum. He was going by the alias Theodore Ramirez, but he is probably going by a different name now. He doesn't like to be alone. He can handle himself in social situations, but once the event is over he finds a way to lure his victims with the intention of keeping them. His victims are asphyxiated and drained of their blood. He removes their internal organs by way of autopsy then fills their torso with different materials as through taxidermy. We believe he is using a chemical cocktail of embalming fluids in order to preserve his victims for as long as he can, so look for someone who possibly works, or had worked in the morgue or a funeral home. He could have been fired for either an overly caring nature toward the dead, or acting strangely aroused," Herring began.

"He can be a little socially awkward at times. One moment he can act like everyone is there to see him, but then he changes to the outcast as though he only went to the party because he knew the cool kids where going to be there and at any moment they will notice he crashed and kick him out," I contributed.

Herring gave me a nod of approval and continued. "Each one of his victims serves a different roll in his life. We feel he is trying to fill the nonexistent family he had as a teenager. He is killing all age ranges as though to fulfill each familial roll. He is approximately thirty years of age, between five nine and six two and about one hundred ninety to two hundred pounds. We assume he is armed and dangerous due to the fact he is able to subdue women *and* men. Now let's get this guy before he decides he needs to have children."

The officers filed out leaving Herring and me behind. She gathered all the information she had and I started to leave.

"Ms. Marcum, could you please try to stay out of the investigation. We are doing what we can to find your friend safe and unharmed. I promise, if we need your help, we will ask," Herring said.

"Look, I will continue looking for Gwen for as long as she is missing. I have a legal conference in a few months. I will quietly do my own investigation and stay out of your way, but when I get back, if I haven't heard any good news, I'm getting right back in your way. I will be calling on a regular basis for any updates on the investigation." I left the room and joined the others.

Eighteen

Three months after Gwendolyn's disappearance, there were still no leads to the whereabouts of Sterling Bigum or Gwen. Every possible lead had been exhausted and we had returned to a semi normal life. Not to say that I hadn't been following a few leads of my own.

Gwen was forced to continue to post her vlogs. I tried to isolate some of the markers in the background of her posts, but came up empty, hoping she was holed up somewhere in a warehouse where I could find her. He always made sure the posts were done in an isolated location and only once at each location. It wouldn't matter if I could figure out where she was, he would have her gone by the time I would have arrived anyway.

I sat at my desk watching her latest vlog posting trying to recognize anything in the background. The camera generally kept close on her face. He never showed she was tied down, but knowing that Gwen always talked with her hands, I could tell.

"Hello all my fans out there in cyber land," her voice was weak. "I am doing well. I miss my friends and family, but don't worry about me. I have someone to protect me from the bad people. To my best friend Anjenette, there was nothing you could do to stop this from happening. To my mother Doreen, go easy on Anjie. She had no knowledge this was going to happen. That is all for now, see you next time."

It had been the only posting she had mentioned us by name. I had also felt it was the only one she wasn't told what to say and she knew how her mother and I would react emotionally. I missed my friend. I told her everything and trusted her more than anyone else in the world. I had to hold on to my secrets without anyone to share them with.

I had stayed in contact with Agent Herring and relayed any information I had learned from the FBI back to Doreen as well. Due to her high volume of phone calls to the police station, Doreen was told if she called one more time to yell at them for not doing their job to her specifications she would be arrested and put in jail for hindering an investigation.

In that time, not only had fifteen bodies been found preserved inside Theodore Ramirez's house, but seventeen others were exhumed from the backyard. An invariable cocktail of drugs had been found in each one of the victims.

He was able to subdue each victim in a way so they were unable to fight back. There weren't any defensive wounds found on the victims. They either didn't or couldn't fight back.

After an extensive investigation through autopsy, the coroner found in each victim where a tube had been inserted into the carotid artery which drained them of their blood. I was told he did it anti-mortem so essentially we assumed he was killing them through exsanguination.

Post-mortem he removed their internal organs through autopsy. The organs were never recovered, so the final report said he either ate them or burned them.

The bodies buried outside appeared to be failed attempts at preservation. The ones inside, must have been successful taxidermy, but the chemicals he used to protect the bodies from decomposing only lasted for a short time before the body rejected it and would begin to decay. The victims' torsos had been filled with different substances as in a poor attempt at taxidermy. The medical examiner informed us that the chemicals he was using were meant to slow down the process of rigor mortis and decomposition. Unfortunately for Sterling, the genetic makeup of each individual is different, so each victim reacted differently to his treatment.

The paper trail for Theodore Ramirez went cold and there wasn't any new information for Sterling Bigum after about a year since his release from prison. While Herring and the other FBI agents along with most of the police department were busy looking for leads, I was looking for Gwen. I knew Sterling had to be the one behind all the madness. I took matters into my own hands and was able to contact his parole officer. He told me his name was Isaac. The only information he was willing to share with me – which was more than I thought was legally allowable – was the date the last time he had heard from Sterling and his last known address.

There was one good thing that came from Theodore Ramirez, Tony Voss. We had been on several dates. All of which went extremely well. Due to the fact that each of us worked so much, we only went out twice per month, but when we were home, we were on the phone with each other.

From our constant conversations, I was able to learn enough about him to know that I really liked him and wanted to spend more time with him. I could only hope that when and if we brought Gwen home, she would be okay with me dating and spending less time with her. Her vlogs were the only thing giving me hope that we could still bring her home alive.

Thankfully, Tony was also a lawyer. He was able to help me follow a few leads. He assisted with the videos and was able to pin point me to a few locations. Nothing really panned out except the blossom of a new relationship.

Due to my heavy work load and trying to find Gwen, I was able to hire a new, fresh out of college, legal assistant named Francine. At first she worked for all the partners and was extremely helpful to everyone. She became my personal assistant once the firm's partners realized she was autistic.

Promising them she could be an asset to the firm, I was responsible for keeping her busy, so she helped me with the investigation of Gwen's disappearance while I worked in order to pay my bills.

Francine went with me to Sterling's last known address, but someone else was living there. A nice older couple had acquired the rental house when Sterling decided to live off the grid.

I knocked and a woman in her mid to late fifties opened the door. The house was approximately twelve hundred square feet with an open floor plan.

"May I help ya?" the woman asked. Her thick Tennessee accent was very prominent.

"My name is Anjenette and this is Francine. We are investigating the disappearance of a man named Sterling Bigum. This is his last known address. Do you happen to know him or where he is?"

"I'm sorry, hon. This house was empty when we moved in. You might wanna talk to the landlord. She may know where he gone."

"Do you happen to have her number or a way I can get in touch with her?" I asked.

"I don't know 'bout that. How 'bout you gimme yer number and I will pass it to her, and she can call ya," the woman suggested.

I complied by handing the woman one of my business cards and Francine and I left. A couple days later I receive a phone call from a woman named Isabelle. She claimed to be the landlord of Sterling's old house.

"My new tenant tells me you have some questions about Sterling Bigum," Isabelle said.

"Yes, ma'am. Do you know when the last time was that you saw him?" I asked.

"Well, he paid his rent for the month on time as usual. I didn't even know he was gone until he missed his rent for the next month. I called and the phone had been disconnected. When I went by the house, it was empty. He was gone. I changed the locks, cleaned the carpet and rented it to the nice couple living there now. Never saw Mr. Bigum again."

"You said you cleaned the carpet. Was there a specific reason?" I asked.

"Normally that is what I do between tenants, but there was a spot on the floor in the bedroom. I had to call professionals to come get the stain out."

"Is there any way I could possibly go into the house and examine the carpet? I would bring an FBI agent with me."

"I don't know. The nice couple living there now is quite settled in and I don't think they would appreciate the invasion," she told me.

"I just feel that if we can figure out what the stain was, we may be able to find out exactly how long he has been killing people," I blurted.

"What do you mean killing people? You told me you were just trying to find out what happened to him, you never said he was a murderer."

I immediately realized my mistake and tried to take it back. "I'm sorry, what I meant to say was, if we can figure out what that stain was we could eliminate the fact that maybe *he* was killed."

"That is not what you said. Are you telling me I allowed a murderer to rent my house and he killed someone inside?"

"I'm not guaranteeing anyone was actually killed in the house, all I'm asking for is to investigate the stain to determine what it could have been."

"No, not going to happen without a warrant. If that FBI agent wants to produce one of those, I would have no choice, but until then I am not allowing access to that house. Now I have to disclose that information to my tenants. Please tell me you did not disclose that to the lovely couple," she argued.

"No ma'am, I did not tell them anything. I'm sorry to have upset you and I'm pretty sure you don't have to tell them anything about that unless they are buying the home," I informed.

"Well, is there anything else I can help you with?" Isabelle asked, apparently trying to change the subject.

"Was there ever a time where he acted strange that you might be able to recall?"

"There was one time he had called me to come over to pick up the rent. He usually dropped it off. When I arrived, he invited me in and offered me something to drink. I noticed him pouring something into the water after he had filled it. Once I saw the cash on the counter I decided it was time to leave. I made up an excuse, grabbed the money, thanked him and bolted out the door. I had no idea what he was spiking that drink with, but I didn't want to stick around to find out. After that, any time he would call me and ask me to come pick up the cash, I would tell him that he could bring it to me whenever he had the time."

"Is that the only time he had done something that seemed odd to you?" I asked.

"Actually no. At one time he had asked how many people lived in the neighborhood. I know that doesn't seem like an odd question. It was his response to the answer that struck me as being odd," Isabelle told me.

"What did he say?"

"He asked if I knew how long it would take for one person to kill them all and if I thought it was possible to be able to get away with it. At the time I thought he was kidding, so I told him the only way he could get away with that would be to kill everyone at the same time, otherwise someone will notice their neighbor missing. I didn't think he was being serious. Now I know he was probably serious."

"Have you checked around the neighborhood to make sure he didn't at least try it?"

"I knocked on a few doors after he moved out just to make sure, but the three houses I went to, everyone answered the door."

"Thank you for taking the time to contact me and answer my questions. You have been most helpful," I told her before hanging up.

I relayed the information to Agent Herring. She wasn't sure if we should bust into someone's home to take samples from an old stain on the carpet, but she thanked me any way. I was sure she was probably tired of hearing from me throughout the last few months.

A week after I spoke with Herring, I found out she was able to obtain the warrant to examine the stain on the carpet from the house. The crime scene investigators had to tear up the carpet and take samples from the carpet pad and weaving since the fibers had been immaculately cleaned.

Two weeks later I was sitting in my office, gathering together several cases to take with me. I was heading out to a legal conference and I was one of the key note speakers.

Because it was at a hotel, Doreen insisted on going with me to keep a watch out for Sterling. She felt as though I would be next if I went alone. I agreed to allow her to come along as long as she didn't get in the way.

I had told Tony the full story of his neighbor and he was having the same reservations as Doreen. I was on the phone convincing him I would be okay when Francine poked her head into my office.

"Anjenette, the car is here to take you to the airport," she told me.

"I'll be right down," I said. She turned to leave and I stopped her. "Hey Francine?"

"Yes," she said, turning back to me.

"Would you like to go with me to this conference?"

"I would be honored. Thank you." Her face lit up. She stepped into my office and began assisting me with gathering the files.

"Tony, I promise I will call you as soon as I get back," I told him before disconnecting the call.

Within minutes we were in the town car headed to my house to grab the bag I had packed for the three day conference. I decided I should call Doreen to inform her I would be running late.

"I have invited my assistant to join us at the conference," I explained.

"Are you sure that is a good idea? If the past has taught us anything it is to be cautious of outsiders. Why would you want to take the risk of endangering yourself?" she lectured.

"I know her and I know she is not going to harm me in any way," I said.

"If the car pulls up to get me and you have been hacked into little pieces, I'm not going."

"Seriously Doreen, sometimes I wonder if you can hear how ridiculous you sound," I told her before hanging up.

"Is everything okay?" Francine asked, as I threw my phone down into my purse.

"That woman is impossible sometimes. I don't know why I allowed her to talk me into permitting her to come along," I said.

"Call her back and tell her you decided you don't want her to come," Francine suggested. "I can protect you."

Francine was uncomfortable being in the car with the driver. I should have known that adding a cranky and frustrated Doreen to the mix would probably send her over the edge.

"No, she sort of has every right to be there. Doreen is kind of like my bodyguard," I said, with a chuckle.

The car pulled up to my house and I ran in and grabbed the bag by the door. I set my new home security system – I had to have it after the incident with Mateo – and darted back to the car.

I climbed back in next to Francine while the driver placed my bag in the trunk. He returned to the driver's seat and headed to Francine's apartment so she could pack. Between the two of us, we were able to have it done in five minutes and were back on the road and headed to pick up Doreen.

She was waiting on her front porch when we pulled up. The driver assisted her with placing her bag into the trunk and we were on our way to the airport.

"Have you heard any news?" Doreen asked as soon as the car started moving.

"I know as much as you know," I told her.

"With your connections, I thought you would be able to get more info."

"The problem is I am connected to this case personally, so no one will give me any more information than they give you."

"I've been able to help," Francine said.

"How have you helped?" Doreen asked.

"I'm not family and I have no emotional connection to the case. I tell them I am studying criminology and this case in particular has intrigued my interest," Francine explained.

"It has worked so far. We were able to get more details about the crime scenes and the fact that there was a second home found filled with taxidermied humans. Don't worry though, Gwen wasn't found at the second home either. Francine has been extremely helpful," I said.

"Wait a minute. Did you just say second house?" Doreen asked, her face turning to an angry shade of red.

"Look, like I said, Gwen wasn't found there either. I figured there was no reason to worry you with minute details if it had nothing to do with Gwen," I told her.

"Why is it you are helping? You have nothing to do with this," Doreen asked, almost with a growl in her voice.

"I like Anjenette. I think she is a good person and I like to think of her as my friend. I always help a friend." Francine's whole demeanor changed. She went from being sweet and quiet to angry and loud.

"I think of you as my friend too, Francine. I appreciate all the help you have provided us with." I turned my focus on Doreen. "You should be grateful for her help. Most of the information I have relayed to you has come from what Francine has received from asking questions."

I turned my focus back to Francine. Lightly touching her hand and looking into her eyes, she mirrored me as I took slow deep breaths. I could feel the tension in her body relax just as the car pulled up to the curb at the airport.

We checked in at the counter, purchased Francine a ticket, went through security and headed for the gate. Francine decided since we had about an hour before the plane would board, she was going to get the three of us coffee.

"What is wrong with her?" Doreen asked as soon as Francine was out of earshot.

"What do you mean? There's nothing wrong with her," I said.

"Why did she just go off on me like that in the car?"

"She likes feeling useful and when you told her she couldn't help, you made her feel useless. The poor girl has been through a lot in her life and needs to feel needed."

"It's almost as though she is not all there," Doreen said, rolling her eyes.

"You know you could be a little more sensitive considering what you've been through. Francine has Asperger's syndrome. She tends to mimic the tone in her voice to the tone in which she is spoken to. She is twenty four and I am trying to give her a stable career, a sense of worth. When she was diagnosed at two years old, her parents decided they couldn't handle it so they gave her up for adoption. She bounced around in foster homes until she was eighteen and moved into a facility where they helped her establish a schedule and get her organized enough to have a job. They even helped her get into college. Give her a break. She's a great girl and a hard worker."

"Asperger's? You mean like autism?" Doreen asked.

"Yes, sometimes she has trouble in social situations, but ever since she has been working with me, I have been able to pull her out of her shell. She is now able to talk to strangers and no longer feels uncomfortable sitting in a room full of people. If there are too many people around though, she won't talk. She puts her headphones on and listens to classical music," I explained.

"You mean like that?" Doreen said, as she pointed to something behind me.

I turned to see Francine standing in the middle of a three way split where passengers for two separate flights were unloading. Friends and family of those passengers were standing around waiting and embracing when they found the one they were looking for. She was surrounded by people, which threw her straight out of her comfort zone and right into fear. I walked over to her. I stood next to her and relaxed. She had her eyes closed and headphones on, so I was sure she would scream and come out swinging if I touched her. I waited for her to notice I was there before proceeding to move her.

Once she opened her eyes and turned her gaze on me, I turned to face her. We were staring into each other's eyes and I could see the fear she possessed. I motioned for her to remove the headphones and she handed me the coffees and complied.

"Remember what we talked about. Don't let the fear take over," I told her.

"I know, I'm supposed to take over the fear," she responded.

"Just focus on me. We are the only two people in the airport. The whole place is deserted." As I spoke, we each took small steps sideways, over to where Doreen sat.

Once we were seated, Francine broke her gaze and closed her eyes. I passed out the coffee cups, one to Doreen and one to Francine, taking a sip from mine. The lady standing over by the closed door preparing to check flight tickets motioned for me to approach her.

"I'll be right back," I said, as I stood.

I walked over to a smiling young lady whose name tag read Katherine. She was holding three boarding passes in her hand and waiving them at me as I stepped up to her.

"That was really sweet what you did for your friend. I understand how hard it is to take someone with special needs into a crowded place. My brother has Asperger's. The social anxiety is the only fall back," she said.

"Francine is a great girl and a hard worker. She just lacks the proper social skills needed. She is also not a fan of being touched," I told her.

"I know what you mean. Look, I called you over here to give you these," she said, handing me the boarding passes.

"These are first class tickets. Why are you giving these to me?" I asked.

"I checked the flight. No one will be in first class so I figured it might be easier on your friend. You will board the plane before anyone else so you won't have to stand in line with a bunch of people around."

"Thank you, but I can't accept these. I didn't pay for them," I informed her, trying to give them back.

"No worries. Coach is overbooked so you were able to get a free upgrade. Trust me; if this is the first time she has ever been on a plane, sitting in coach will not be fun. Enjoy first class and take care of your friend. The plane will be boarding soon," Katherine said, with a smile so big I was sure her face hurt.

"Well, thank you. I appreciate it," I said, heading back over to my seat.

"What did she want?" Doreen asked, as soon as I sat down.

"We were upgraded to first class," I told her, handing her one of the tickets.

"Upgraded? Why?"

I jabbed a thumb in Francine's direction.

Doreen shrugged and smiled. "Maybe she can be useful."

I rolled my eyes.

Fifteen minutes later we were on the plane headed toward our destination.

Nineteen

The plane ride was smooth. We were the only three passengers in first class, which helped Francine relax. When the plane landed, we were the first to exit, so there wasn't a big crowd as we walked through the jet bridge. Once we made it to the terminal, there was a gentleman waiting with a sign that read 'Anjenette Marcum'. I felt important seeing my name on a sign.

"I'm Anjenette Marcum," I introduced myself.

"I hope your flight was pleasant," the man said, as he reached for my luggage.

I passed my bag to him to carry, then said, "It was fantastic."

He led us out to an awaiting limousine. The three of us acted as though it was a normal occurrence for us to ride in limos until we were inside and the doors were closed.

"Oh my goodness, this is awesome. I can't believe the law firm sent a limo to pick us up. How cool is this?" I said, touching everything I could get my hands on like a child would.

"I've never been in a limo before," Francine said, with a look of awe and amazement.

"You two need to calm down and act in a professional manner, because the driver is coming. But yes, this is awesome," Doreen agreed.

When the driver opened his door and slid in behind the wheel, we composed ourselves back into the same nonchalant adults we were before we got into the car.

"I have been instructed to drop you off at the hotel. Is there anywhere else you ladies would like to go before that?" the driver asked.

"No, thank you. We would like to go straight to the hotel to freshen up," I said, in a rich snooty woman tone.

The driver nodded his head, shifted the car into drive and headed off toward the hotel.

The room we were staying in was larger than the one Gwen and I stayed in for our mini-vacation. Just inside the door to the right was the bathroom. On the other side of the bathroom wall was a fold out sofa bed, which Doreen elected to take because it was closest to the door. A small corridor separated the sofa and a two foot counter with a mini-fridge nestled underneath. There was a partial wall separating two double beds as if it were its own room. A large dresser was placed along the wall across from the beds. There was one nightstand between the beds and a small writing desk next to the dresser.

Francine set her luggage down on the first bed and I set mine on the second. I placed my briefcase down on the desk and opened it up. Extracting two folders, I handed one to each of them.

It was a copy of the itinerary for the conference for the next day. I wanted to make sure they would know where I was at all times. I expected Francine to accompany me to each speaking opportunity, but Doreen would need to wait in the lobby.

"There is an hour and a half gap between the first expo and the second. We can grab a bite to eat and I can change my clothes if needed," I said.

"I have a list of possible high risk areas here in the hotel. There is a blind spot near the elevators. A tree is stationed in a small notch cut out between two elevators. The one on the right goes down to the underground parking garage and the one on the left goes up to the rooms. There is a bathroom near there, so if you go anywhere by them for any reason, don't go alone," Doreen said handing Francine and me a list of five possible areas I could be abducted.

"When did you get this list?" I asked, knowing she had been with Francine and me the entire time since we had arrived.

"I flew here last week and checked out the entire hotel to make sure each blind spot was accounted for."

"Seems like you've gone a little overboard, doesn't it?" Francine asked.

"My daughter was abducted from a hotel. I am taking every precaution so it doesn't happen to someone else's daughter. Mr. and Mrs. Marcum are friends of mine and I am doing everything in my power to keep their child safe," Doreen scolded.

"Since when have my parents ever been your friends? You blamed me for Gwen's disappearance and them for encouraging us to take the vacation. I don't understand why you are trying to protect me," I said.

"You always treated Gwen like a sister and your parents treated her like a daughter. When she was abducted, the three of you banded together to help find her. I respect all of you for that and I'm sorry if I ever made you feel otherwise." Doreen's eyes filled with tears as she spoke.

"Thank you for that. We all loved her like family." I walked over to where she stood and hugged her.

"Now if we are done with all this family love, I would like to discuss tomorrow's events," Francine said, harshly.

Doreen opened her mouth to say something, but I stopped her by giving her a look that said, 'Just let it go'.

"Francine, I'm going to have you with me at each seminar. Doreen, because you don't work for a law firm and you are technically here to be my bodyguard, you aren't allowed in the lecture rooms. You can do whatever you want until we are done," I explained

"I am going to keep an eye on all the people entering that room," Doreen informed.

"I don't know if I feel comfortable with being in a room full of people," Francine said.

"You can bring your headphones so if you feel overwhelmed, you can calm yourself. I won't be sitting with you the whole time, which means I won't be there to soothe your fears," I told Francine.

"This is ridiculous. I don't understand why you would want someone who is socially awkward in the room with you. What good does that do?" Doreen complained.

"Are you upset because *you* can't come in the room with me?" I asked Doreen, with a condescending tone.

"That's not what I'm saying. I'm just thinking it would be easier to keep a look out if there were a second set of eyes. That's all," Doreen said.

"We can't be too sure of what Sterling looks like right now. Even the FBI is circulating several different photos of him. Long hair, short hair, full facial hair, partial facial hair, no facial hair. No one is sure how or if he has changed his appearance."

I glanced over at Francine who was now sitting in the center of her bed, listening to her music with her eyes closed. Deciding we were done for the night, I slowly climbed on her bed and she opened her eyes.

I motioned for her to take off her headphones. She complied and I gently placed my hand on her knee.

"We are done, it's over. Let's try to get some sleep. We have a big day ahead of us," I told her.

She nodded and we settled in for the night.

The next morning, Francine was already up before Doreen and me and she had ordered breakfast. A food cart with assorted fruits, a couple of stacks of pancakes, three plates of eggs, three glasses of orange juice, three glasses of milk and a carafe of coffee accompanied by three mugs, had been brought into the room.

I picked at the fruit and poured me a cup of coffee. Once I noticed the time, I guzzled what was left in my mug and headed for the bathroom in order to quickly shower and dress for the day.

The three of us were ready to walk out the door by seven a.m. so I could check in by seven thirty for my first speaking arrangement at eight.

"I will be out around eleven, but I have to be back by twelve thirty," I told both Francine and Doreen, as we stood outside the lecture hall.

"I will be right here keeping watch for any suspicious characters," Doreen said, handing Francine a photo of Sterling. "If you see this man inside, please let me know."

Francine saluted as if she had been given orders from her drill instructor. Doreen rolled her eyes.

Francine and I entered the lecture hall and found our seats in the front row with the name of the law firm on the back. I told her to stay in her seat while I schmoosed with the other speakers before we got started.

As the attendees began to arrive, the room filled up quickly. I scanned the room for anyone who looked out of place, but everyone seemed to appear comfortable.

I excused myself from the group of professionals and sat down next to Francine.

"Doreen is going a little overboard with thinking you're going to be the next to be abducted, don't you think? I mean, if the guy was obsessed with your friend, why would he take you?" Francine whispered, as everyone continued to mingle.

I was proud to see her using what I called her private bubble. It was a tactic I came up with to help with her fear of being in a room full of people. As long as I was with her, her private bubble surrounded us both and we were secluded from everyone else. It only worked if she set all her focus on me and no one else spoke directly to either of us, which would break her concentration.

"Technically, I won't be the next. Gwendolyn has been missing for four months and in that time twelve more people that we know of have disappeared. She is just being cautious. Both Gwen and I knew Sterling. If he wanted to taunt me any more than he already has, that would be the way to do it," I replied. "If he is trying to keep Gwen and wants her alive, then he knows if he has me, she would stay with him."

"You have to think positive. I can't imagine…," Francine couldn't finish her sentence.

"Well, well, well. Look who's here to represent Shoney, Styles and Staff," a familiar male voice interrupted our conversation.

"Well, if it isn't the creep himself, Mateo Cray. How did you get in to this conference? You don't work for a law firm. Not only that, but you can't represent the law if you break the law." My hands began to shake as I stood in order to be eye to eye with the man who had tried to kill me. "Speaking of the law, when did you get out of jail?"

"I work with Stevens, Oppenheim and Taft. They pay me to dig up dirt on the prosecution. Kind of like a private investigator. All I need is a camera and a notebook. They also helped me get paroled. Must be you have been too busy to check your mail for the invitation to my parole hearing, seeing as how you weren't there."

Mateo stood with an undefined arrogance as though he knew I would be there. The smug smile on his face told me he weaseled his way into the conference in order to make sure he ran into me.

I felt relief when the announcer stood at the podium and asked everyone to take their seats. I was nervous to see Mateo there and was worried I wouldn't even be able to get through my speech.

Francine noticed my apprehension and handed me my note cards. Written on each one was a topic along with major points about each topic I planned to present. Thank goodness for Francine. She always knew what I needed.

I looked over my notes and ran my entire lecture in my head as the first speaker stepped up to the podium. I didn't hear anything that was said until the announcer said my name.

I stood, composed myself, then headed up to the front of the room. Reminding myself 'I'm a professional', I was surprised at how well I was able to get through my hour with Mateo staring at me the whole time.

Twenty

When the first lecture was over, Francine and I were able to slip out of the room before we ran into Mateo again. We met up with Doreen in the lobby.

"I thought you were going to be waiting outside the room?" Francine wondered.

"I was told I couldn't be there while the lecture was going on. When I tried to explain why I was standing guard, they said they would call security if I didn't remove myself," Doreen explained, sounding like a child whose siblings didn't want to play with her.

Francine and I laughed as Doreen looked down at her hands.

"I'm sorry. I don't mean to laugh, but did mommy make you milk and cookies to make you feel better?" Francine mocked.

"Okay, that's enough. I need to go to the ladies room. I'll be right back," I said, excusing myself. "Can the two of you be nice to each other for a few minutes?"

"Let me go with you," Francine said, shooting a mean look at Doreen.

"No, I'll be fine. I'm only going to be a few minutes."

Francine sat down on one of the leather chairs in the lobby. Feeling the need to splash water on my face, I headed toward the lavatory. Seeing Mateo again had me more nervous than if I were to have seen Sterling and to my knowledge, Mateo hadn't actually killed anyone.

As I approached the bathroom door, Mateo appeared in front of me. He licked his lips, wiggled his caterpillar like eyebrows and looked me up and down.

"Looking good, Anjenette," he said, blocking my path.

"Mateo please, just let me pass." My hands were trembling again.

"A little hot thing like you shouldn't be alone. Something could happen and no one would know."

"Is that another threat?"

"Oh honey, if I was threatening you, I would have told you I have a knife in my pocket and I am planning to use it to mess up that pretty little face of yours. You had me arrested and thrown in jail. I have been waiting for this moment for months. I liked you and you turned me down every time I tried to ask you out."

"I had you arrested because you broke into my house. What did you think I was going to do? Thank you for breaking the dead bolts and locking me in with a psychopath," I said, a lump forming in my throat as I remembered the fear I felt the night he had invaded my home.

"I just want an apology," he replied.

"An apology for what?"

"For turning all the other women in your office against me."

"You did that all on your own."

I tried to push past him and he reached for his pocket with one hand and grabbed my arm with the other. I felt the sting as he sliced open my forearm from elbow to wrist. Blood poured from the wound and he let me go. I ran into the bathroom and began running water over my arm. The door swung opened and Francine stepped in.

"Oh my goodness! What happened to you?" she asked looking at the bloody mess on the floor and in the sink.

"Mateo cornered me outside in the hall and pulled a knife on me," I explained, trying to hold back the tears burning my eyes.

"We need to get you to the hospital and contact the police. You could need stiches," she said, grabbing as many paper towels as she could.

"No way, no hospitals. I don't need a paper trail leading to me here if Sterling is trying to find me. When I get home I'll talk to my attorney and file charges, but for now let's just try to stop the bleeding," I instructed, as I pulled my arm back from the water and placed the paper towels Francine was holding over the gaping wound.

"Your clothes are covered in blood and the gash on your arm is going to be noticeable at your next lecture. Not only that, but what if Mateo shows up to the next lecture and he tries something in front of everyone?"

"I'm sure the hotel here has a first aid kit. I can wrap it up and I have a change of clothes upstairs in the room. There, problem solved. Now let's go," I said, heading toward the door.

"Fine, but I'm not going to let you out of my sight from now on. Where you go, I go," Francine said, following so close behind me if I would have stopped, she would have stepped on the heel of my shoe.

"What happened?" Doreen asked, as we approached the lobby.

"Mateo Cray is here. He is an attendee at the conference," I told Doreen.

Francine helped me onto a chair and ran to the front counter.

"Mateo Cray? Is he the one who broke into your house a few months ago?" Doreen asked.

"That's the one," I told her, as Francine returned with the desk clerk who was carrying a first aid kit.

"What happened? Do you want me to call an ambulance, or the police?" she asked.

"That's not necessary," I told her.

"How did this happen?" she asked.

"I'm just so clumsy sometimes," I said, pretending I did it myself somehow.

"This is going to sting a bit, but it should help stop the bleeding," she said, producing a spray bottle of antiseptic.

I pealed back the paper towels, which had begun to stick to my arm as the blood coagulated. As I exposed the wound to the air, I felt a tingling sensation radiate through my arm as blood was still seeping from the gash. When she sprayed the antiseptic, pain emanated through my body. I bit down on my bottom lip and squeezed the arm of the chair to keep from screaming.

The desk clerk used gauze to clean up most of the blood. I pinched the skin closed to cover as much of the exposed muscle as possible.

"Do you have butterfly bandages or Band-Aids? Just put something over it to close it together and wrap some gauze around my arm. I'll be fine."

Francine and the desk clerk looked at each other. Shrugging, they did exactly as I had requested. Francine attempted to hold the wound closed while the clerk stuck large Band-Aids along my arm to hold it in place.

"Are you sure about this, Anjenette?" Francine asked, after my arm had been wrapped up.

"There is no way you did this to yourself. I have to alert the police," the desk clerk said, returning to her post behind the counter and picking up the phone.

"Yes, Francine. There is no reason to alarm anyone. Let me just go change my clothes so I can look presentable at the Q and A portion of the conference and this day can be over," I said.

"If you go up to the room, we are going with you," Doreen said, standing.

"No, just wait here since she is calling the police. Keep a look out for Mateo and Sterling. I should be back by the time an officer arrives. I'll have the concierge or someone walk me up," I suggested.

"As long as you don't go alone," Doreen told me.

"Don't worry. I'm going to change my clothes and clean up a bit. I promise I won't be long."

They watched as I walked over to the concierge desk and requested an escort to my room. The man seated behind the desk stared at me a moment before lifting the receiver of the phone in front of him. I knew he wanted to know why I was covered in blood, but he didn't ask.

"Could you please send a bellhop to the concierge desk?" he spoke to the person on the other end of the line. "Thank you."

He hung up the phone and looked back at me. He attempted a smile, but I could tell he was dying to know what happened to me.

"Someone should be right out to walk you to your room," he informed me.

"Thank you, sir. You have been most gracious," I said and curtsied.

I glanced over to see Doreen and Francine still watching me. I waived, they waived back. A young gentleman, of about eighteen, approached me. He was dressed in a grey suit with a red bellman's hat. He almost looked like one of those dancing monkeys for a street performer.

"Ma'am, how may I assist you?" the bellhop, whose nametag read William, asked. His eyes almost bulged from their sockets as he noticed my clothing.

"Would you be so kind as to escort me to my room, please? There are a lot of crazy people in the world and I don't want to become a victim," I told him, in a stereotypical rich lady voice.

"I would be happy to," he answered.

I could tell by the look on his face, he knew I had already encountered one of the crazy people. We headed over to the elevators and the whole time I could see him from my peripherals staring at me.

"So, William, what do you want to be when you grow up?" I asked, making idle chit chat while we waited for the elevator to arrive.

"What I really want to be is a musician," he said, his face beaming.

"Really, a musician? Well, isn't that interesting," I said, as the elevator stopped at the lobby floor.

"Oh yeah. I can play the guitar and the bass. Some people think that they are the same, but they're not. A guitar has six strings while the bass only has four. I'm trying to save up for a drum set so I can have friends come over and we can start practicing and be a real rock band," William rambled, as we rode the lift up.

The elevator arrived at the floor. We began walking down the hallway toward the room.

"Well, it sounds like you have a great dream William. Don't let anyone stop you from achieving it," I told him, as we stopped in front of the room and I slid the key card into the slot on the door.

"Thank you ma'am, I won't."

"And thank you for walking me to my room. We will have to do this again sometime. Have a musical afternoon," I told him, as I presented him with a twenty dollar bill.

"Good bye, ma'am," William said, as I closed the door.

"What a sweet kid," I said, heading to the bathroom.

I pealed my clothes off as gently as I could so as not to disturb the bandaging on my arm. Reaching for a wash cloth, I turned on the water faucet and allowed it to run in order to retrieve warm water.

Once the water had reached the desired temperature, I placed the cloth beneath the stream to wet it. I wiped down every part of my body where there was dried blood.

I heard the key card enter and exit the slot in the door as well as the door open and close. I assumed Francine and Doreen decided they would escort the police to the room after they noticed the bell hop return to the lobby. I ran the wash cloth underneath the water again and washed my face.

I reapplied my make-up and stepped out into the room to get a change of clothes to dress in. Looking around, I didn't see any one. I was sure I heard the door close.

"Francine? Doreen?" I called out, but there was no answer.

I decided the sounds I heard may have come from the room next door. Pulling a grey skirt suit from my garment bag, I dressed quickly. As soon as I had zipped up the back of my skirt, I felt a sharp object being pressed into my back.

"Turn around and I'll slit your throat," a man's voice said from behind me.

I tensed up. The voice was familiar, but I was sure it wasn't Mateo. I didn't make any sudden movements as he guided me toward the exit. He opened the door to the room just enough so he could peer out into the hallway. As he poked his head out, he pressed my face against the wall so I was looking into the room.

There wasn't a single person wandering the hall, so he led me out the door and down the corridor toward the stairwell. We walked down the few flights of stairs through the hotel, then one more flight of stairs into the parking garage below the hotel.

"What do you want?" I asked, as we walked past several rows of cars.

Without an answer, he led me over to the back of a blue four door sedan and opened the trunk.

"Get in," he ordered, pressing the sharp object harder into my back. It was at that point I realized he had a knife. I could feel the knife pierce through my skin and blood began to trickle down my back and pool around my waist band.

I climbed in and lay down. Just before the trunk closed I looked at his face. I knew exactly who he was.

Twenty-One

'Sterling Bigum broke into my hotel room to abduct me. That must be how he got Gwendolyn. Maybe he worked for the hotel chain and had a master key card,' I thought.

I was in the trunk of Sterling's car. My first thought was to figure a way out. As I felt around for the safety release handle to open the trunk, my mind suddenly wandered to Gwendolyn and I realized I could finally find out what happened to her.

Lying in the dark trunk, I was missing my most important sense, sight. Feeling around me, I tried to find some type of weapon. There was nothing within reach. I figured it had to be underneath the carpeted board I was laying on. Unfortunately, it was too stiff for me to lift up and reach under while I was laying on it.

Trying to feel the motion of the vehicle, I concentrated on every bump in the road, and counted every time he stopped, in order to remember how many times and which direction he turned.

When he had reached his destination, he turned off the engine. I knew it was the final stop. I heard the car door slam shut and knew he was coming to the back of the vehicle to retrieve me.

When the hatch opened, the sunlight poured in. I was squinting and blinking as much as I could in order to adjust my eyes from total darkness to bright light, when Sterling reached in and pulled me out by my hair.

"Owe, Sterling please, let go," I pleaded.

Looking around at the surrounding area, I realized we were in a residential neighborhood. I imagined the neighbors we had interviewed from the house registered to Theodore Ramirez. Unfortunately, there wasn't a single person outside, or driving down the street, so no one noticed him retrieving someone from the trunk of his car.

"Scream and I'll gut you right here on my front lawn," he said, guiding me to the front door of his house.

"Why are you doing this Sterling?" I asked, as he shoved me into the house.

"Sterling Bigum no longer exists. This month I'm Edward Nilsen," he said, with a smug look on his face.

Inside the home, the foyer was a small hallway that dead ended after about fifteen feet. There was an opening to the left and a door to the right at the dead end.

He ushered me to the left at the end of the hallway. It opened into the living room. I could see two men sitting on a sofa, but they never turned around. I could only see the back of their heads.

A little further in was the dining room and kitchen. In the kitchen there was a woman, with her back to me, cooking at the stove. She had long dark hair and like the others, she never turned in our direction.

"Please, someone help me," I said, as he pressed down on my shoulders, forcing me to sit on one of the chairs at the dining room table.

He began to strap me down with leather straps. He pulled the bindings so tight, I could feel pain radiate through my body from the gash Mateo inflicted.

"They can't help you. They only obey my commands." He walked over to the woman in the kitchen and moved her as though she were a mannequin.

He stood her in front of the table as if he were having her watch me. Her face appeared to have been molded into the expression frozen on her face.

She used to be real, I could tell that, but now she was stuffed like an animal. He had figured out a way to keep people from leaving. I was afraid that was exactly what he had done with Gwendolyn, but she wasn't there that I could see.

"This is Darla. She cooks for me. Tom and Jerry in there watch television with me. They are my friends. Everyone, say hello to Anjenette. She is going to be staying with us for a while," he said, with a sort of childish tone and kissed Darla on the cheek.

"You're crazy," I said, struggling under the restraints.

I attempted to pull my arms free, but all that did was cause the wound to start bleeding again. The white gauze was now stained red. I winced in pain.

"Now look what you did. I'm going to have to clean you up. I don't want you bleeding to death until I'm ready," he said, retrieving a first aid kit from the kitchen.

He unstrapped my wounded arm. As soon as it was free, I swung at him as hard as I could and punched him square in the jaw. The blow knocked him off balance, which only pissed him off. He stood over me and with all his might, punched me on the side of my head.

"You stupid bitch," Sterling said to me, rubbing his jaw. "You should feel so lucky that you are still alive. If my Gwendolyn hadn't of asked for you, I would have already killed you."

I felt disoriented. My eyes were unable to focus on anything distinctive. I could feel his hands on my arm as he unwrapped the gauze and removed the bandages. He was rough as he wiped the blood clean from my skin. He was scrubbing it as though he were sanding a piece of wood. 'He said Gwenie asked for me. That must mean she is still alive,' I thought.

"Just relax and let me help you," he said, with a caring tone.

I blinked, in an attempt to focus on what he was doing. He produced a sewing needle and thread. I watched as he threaded the needle. With one hand, he pinched together my skin to hold the wound closed. With the other, he proceeded to sew the epidermis together.

Luckily, the pain had practically numbed my arm and the blow he inflicted upon me still had me out of it enough, I didn't quite feel the needle enter my skin. Once he had finished stitching me up, he again scrubbed the wound.

"You're crazy," I told him, again.

"I'm NOT crazy!" he yelled at me, then his tone changed. "I'm clever. You got to spend the last eight years with the love of my life and during that time I have perfected my craft."

He finished off my arm by wrapping clean gauze around the affected area. Not only did the wound burn, but my arm was also raw from being scrubbed so hard. Returning the first aid kit to the kitchen, he retrieved a different kit from the same cabinet.

When he returned to the table, he set down the box, strapped my arm back down to the chair, then opened the box. Inside that kit were syringes, vials, lotions and creams. He picked up a vial filled with an ember colored substance. Turning the vial upside down, inserting the needle of the syringe, he extracted some of the liquid.

He placed the vial back into the box, then turned to focus on Darla. He injected her with the substance in several places on her body. Once the syringe was empty, he grabbed one of the bottles of lotion and stood it up on the table. Using the hand pump, he expelled a fair amount, then proceeded to rub lotion on all her body parts not covered with clothing.

He retreated to the living room with the kit and performed the same ritual on Tom and Jerry. As he rubbed them down, I struggled with my one good arm, trying to loosen the leather strap. The more I struggled, the more raw my wrist became. I gave up for a while and looked around. I wanted to remember my surroundings so when I escaped, I could tell the police where he was.

I didn't see a single window inside the house. I remembered at least three from the outside. I figured he must have dry walled over them to keep people from seeing what he was doing inside his house of horrors.

"Tom, Jerry, this is Anjie. Soon she will be our new friend. I have special plans for her, but not as special as what I had planned for Gwendolyn." He paused as though he was listening to them respond. "Tom, I think that would be inappropriate. I will think about it though. She does look like a lively one."

He took his injection kit and put it back into the cabinet where he had retrieved it from. I tried to pull my arm free from the restraint to no avail.

"Tom thinks you're pretty," Sterling said, in his childish tone, smiling. "If you're good, I will let you spend some time with him. I know how long it has been since you were with a man. Just don't gossip with Darla about what you end up doing with him. They used to be an item."

"You're sick and it is none of your business how long it has been for me."

"I have been watching Gwendolyn since my parole and I know you have only been around her. I've seen everything."

"What did you do to Gwen?" I finally asked, tears forming in my eyes.

"All in good time sweetheart. Oh, and if you're wondering, yes, she is still alive. That is, until she gives birth."

"What did you do, you sick son of a bitch," I said through clenched teeth.

"Gwen and I talked about having a family when we were in high school. Then my little faux pas happened and she was ripped from my life. I finally had the opportunity to take her when y'all went on that vacation and I seized the moment.

"Once I had her, she begged for you. I told her I needed to find a new house somewhere far away from the Theodore Ramirez house. I knew if the police were able to find that house, it was only a matter of time before they found the Dennis Ridgeway house. By then I was already going by a different name, but I was still too close. If I were to go out in public, someone might recognize me and blow my cover. The people at Ted's house were just a trial run. I couldn't keep them preserved long enough to keep out the stench. I had to rethink my approach. When I came up with Dennis, his approach at preservation was better, but it was too close to Ted. John Bernardo was only the next town over, still too close." His tone was somber, almost as though he were pleased with himself.

"What did you do with her?" I yelled at him.

"I'm getting to it," he yelled back. He took two deep breaths, calmed down and changed his tone to continue. "Like I said, she begged for you. When I mentioned I needed a place far away, she told me you were coming here for a conference and with the time frame, I had just enough time to settle in before grabbing you. When you left the airport, I followed you to the hotel. I thought it was only poetic to abduct you the same way I took Gwen. By the way, you won't have to worry about the guy who did that to you," he said, referring to my arm.

"You fucking asshole. You are never going to get away with this," I yelled, hoping someone could hear me.

"I already have gotten away with it several times before. This is my sixth house under a different alias. Each house had a total of fifteen friends inside and the ones who didn't make it were buried outside."

"What did you do to Mateo?"

"Is that what his name is? What a stupid ass name. Besides, I thought you would be happy if I got rid of that guy?"

"I never wanted him dead. I just wanted him to leave me alone," I said, relaxing under my bindings. I was giving up the struggle.

"Now, he will leave you alone, forever," Sterling said, smiling.

Twenty-Two

It was almost as though he had two personalities. When he talked about Gwen, he had a certain mature tone. It was as if they were together in a grown up relationship consensually.

The change in his tone was when he was talking about those he called his friends. It was childish, almost as though he had reverted back to when he was in fifth grade.

"If she is still alive, I want to see her," I told him.

"I will take you to her, but you can only talk to her."

He unstrapped me from the chair and led me to the other side of the house. Tom and Jerry continued to sit on the sofa facing the television. I knew they wouldn't turn, but I continued to watch.

Sterling opened the door on the other side of the hallway. It opened to a bedroom. On the bed, Gwen lay there tied to the headboard and footboard. I ran to the side of the bed and stroked her hair. She turned her head and opened her eyes.

"Anjenette?" she said with a weak tone. "What are you doing here?"

"He got me too." I leaned in to whisper in her ear. "We are going to get out of here."

"That's enough. Let's go," Sterling said, grabbing me by the arm and pulling me out of the room.

"NO!" Gwen screamed. "Please don't leave me alone in here anymore."

"Please Sterling, let me stay with her. I can take care of her and make sure your baby is born healthy," I begged.

"Fine, but you can't untie her."

He threw me back into the room and closed the door. I fell to my hands and knees and crawled over, returning to her bedside.

"Did he hurt you?" I asked her.

"Physically no, emotionally yes. He raped me every day for a month. He told me he wanted to make sure that a part of me lived on after I was gone. He is planning to kill me after the baby is born." Gwen's eyes were red rimmed and tears were flowing onto her pillow.

"I'm not going to let anything happen to you. I will find a way out of here," I told her.

I walked over to the door and turned the knob. It was locked from the outside. I banged on the door and called out for Sterling. Within moments he opened the door.

"What do you want?" he asked.

"Can she get some water and food? If you want a healthy baby, he or she needs to have proper nutrition and regular meals," I said pretending I was there to help him.

"I'll have Darla bring you something." He pushed me out of the way and slammed the door closed.

"Who's Darla?" Gwen asked.

"He has three dead people out there he is keeping preserved for his own sick game," I told her, staring at the bedroom door attempting to figure a way out.

"I'm sorry I brought you into this."

"No you didn't. He did this. I am here because of him," I comforted her, walking over to her bedside.

"I told him where you were going to be and when. I asked for you. You are only here because I asked him to bring you to me."

"Tell me what happened after you left the hotel restaurant," I asked her.

"When I went upstairs to the hotel room, he was right behind me. I could feel his presence as he followed me to the room. I didn't know it was him, I just had the feeling I was being followed. When I stopped in front of the door, he continued down the hall past me. I assumed my paranoia was unfounded so I went inside and closed the door," she told me.

"If you were feeling uncomfortable, why didn't you lock the door from the inside?" I asked.

"I knew you would be coming up soon and I didn't want to lock you out. I just grabbed some clothes to change into and went into the bathroom. I heard the door and thought it was you. I finished dressing and reached for the door knob. As soon as I opened the door, he was standing right there on the other side. He grabbed me and I tried to hold onto the door, but he over powered me. The bathroom door slammed shut and he was squeezing me as tight as he could in his arms. He had one arm around my waist and his other hand covered my mouth. I struggled; I promise I struggled as much as I could. He slammed my head into the wall and I felt so disoriented I could no longer fight him," she explained.

"This is not your fault. Don't blame yourself. This is my fault. I should have left with you."

"He planned this. Neither one of us could have predicted he was still obsessing over me."

"Where did he take you?" I asked.

"First, we went to a house with upwards of about twenty people posed like mannequins throughout the whole place. He introduced me to all of them as his wife. It was so weird. Every day he raped me and the next morning he would force me to take a pregnancy test. When it finally came up positive, he told me we were going to be a family. I told him I needed you to be with me through the pregnancy. He told me the police were getting closer and in order for me to have you we needed to move further away.

"I thought that if the police became too close to catching him he might kill me in order to get away. I explained to him about the conference. I knew you would be there. So, he packed the two of us up and moved here. When we arrived I said if he wanted to be a real family he had to leave his friends behind. No more bringing new people into the house. He agreed and allowed me to wander the house. Every day I was given chores to do to keep me busy. I tried to escape once so he tied me to this bed. I didn't know he was still killing people," she told me.

"We are going to get out of here and we can deal with your situation then, but until that happens we have to pretend as though we are on board with his mission."

"How are we going to get out of here? This door automatically locks when he closes it. There are no windows in here. There is no way out."

There was a knock on the door and it opened. Just on the other side stood Darla. She was holding a tray of food. Her expression was still frozen in the same dead look she had earlier. I took the tray from her and began walking back to the bed. The door slammed behind me.

I walked over and set the tray down on the bedside table. Sitting down on the bed next to Gwen, I proceeded to untie her hands from the headboard.

Before I could finish untying the first knot, the door swung open and Sterling came rushing in wielding a knife. Gwen screamed as he grabbed me by my hair and pulled me up into a standing position with my back against him and the knife resting on my throat.

"I thought we had a deal. You can't untie her," he said, his lips touching my ear.

"I just figured it would be easier for her to eat if she wasn't tied up."

"You can feed her." He moved the knife away from my throat and shoved me.

I landed face down on the bed across Gwen's legs. I moved slowly into a sitting position.

"She is a grown up Sterling. Don't you think she could feed herself?"

"Fine, but when she's done, you must tie her back to the bed."

He left the room, slamming the door behind him. I leaned over and proceeded to untie Gwen's hands. Her arms had been hanging from the headboard for so long she was having trouble controlling the muscles to do what she wanted.

I helped her move her left arm so it rested across her lap, then maneuvered to the other side of the bed to untie her right arm. Before handing her the tray of food, I untied her feet from the footboard and helped her bend her knees and move her arms so she could pull herself up into a sitting position.

I rested the tray on her lap and assisted her with eating. She couldn't quite get her hands all the way to her mouth. Once the blood circulation had returned to her limbs, she was able to feed herself without my assistance.

A few moments later we heard the front door to the house slam shut. Sterling had left us alone.

"Do you think he's coming back?" Gwen asked with a mouth full of food.

"Of course he's coming back. Now is the time for me to find the camera."

"How do you know there's a camera in here?"

"He knew I was untying you. There has to be a way he can see in here."

I checked all the little knick knacks for small holes where a camera could be hidden. I didn't see anything. Walking over and leaning against the foot of the bed, I looked up at the ceiling and spotted an air vent.

I stepped over to the bed side table, picked up the lamp and clock that occupied it and set them on the floor. Proceeding to move the stand, I pulled it over underneath the vent and climbed on top of it.

Placing my feet flat on the table, I stood up. Between the slats of the vent, I could see the red record light flashing. I climbed down and attempted to locate an implement to use to remove the vent cover.

While I was rummaging through the room, the front door closed again. I quickly moved the table back to its place next to the bed and replaced the lamp and clock.

Twenty-Three

Gwen and I listened as two voices echoed through the house. One was undoubtedly Sterling's. The second was an unknown female.

We weren't sure how long he had been gone, but I was sure Sterling would be angry to see Gwen was still free. I picked up the tray from her lap and set it down on the nightstand.

"I have to tie you back to the bed before he comes in here," I told her.

"Okay, but can you make sure the bindings are loose so I can move around some?" she agreed.

She readied herself and I started with her hands. Just as I was finishing with her feet, the door flew open. Sterling appeared in the doorway.

"Anjenette, come with me," he said.

"What about Gwen?" I asked, not wanting to leave her side.

"She'll be fine for about an hour."

He grabbed my arm and dragged me through the house leaving the door to the bedroom open. There was a door, which I thought was a pantry, just past the kitchen on one wall of the dining room.

He pulled me through the door. It was a torture chamber. A metallic table was in the center of the room. A woman lay strapped to the table, naked. Indisputably, it was the woman whose voice was heard arguing with Sterling earlier.

"I want you to help me with this," he told me with complete seriousness.

"I'm not going to help you kill someone," I told him.

"Kill someone! You're going to kill me?" the woman on the table yelled.

"If you don't help me, I'll gut you right here," he said angrily, ignoring his victim. Then, changing his tone to calm said, "and no one will ever know what happened to you or Gwen. I will make sure neither of your bodies is found."

"Please don't kill me," the woman pleaded. "I don't want to die. Please let me go. I won't tell anyone, I promise."

Sterling stroked her hair. "Of course you won't tell anyone. In a matter of minutes, you won't even be able to speak."

I started to cry and stepped up next to the metal table. I looked down at the poor girl and mouthed, 'I'm sorry'.

"Please, help me," she said, in a low tone.

Sterling handed me a pair of surgical gloves. I pulled them on as he pulled on a pair of his own. He set up a rolling tray next to me with several needles and vials along with a scalpel.

"Hand me the succinylcholine," he said once he took his place on the other side of the table.

"Which one is that?" I asked.

"It is the first vial on the tray. Everything is in order," he explained, sounding frustrated.

"What is it going to do?" I asked, as I handed him the vial and syringe.

"It is going to relax every muscle in her body, including those needed to breathe, until she suffocates to death."

"Please, no! Just shoot me or at least make it quick," the woman suggested.

Sterling continued to ignore her as he extracted the succinylcholine with the syringe. He flicked the needle a couple of times and gently pressed the plunger to release any air. Tying a tourniquet around her upper arm, he pulled it tight and prepared the vein along her antecubital. Once the cephalic vein protruded from her skin, Sterling plunged the syringe into her blood stream.

She yelled out in pain. Tears poured from her eyes. "Please, help me," she pleaded with me.

I looked into her eyes and could see her fear, feel her pain. Sterling removed the tourniquet and disposed of the syringe while I watched the drug take effect. As she struggled to free herself, her movements began to slow down almost as though she were moving in slow motion, until she stopped moving all together. Her breathing slowed down and she lay there completely paralyzed. I cried for her. In a way I was mourning her death.

He grabbed a pair of scissors that were placed on the table next to her. Gripping her shirt in his fist, he spread the scissor blades. Placing one blade under her shirt, one above, he cut her shirt off her body. Next, he cut off her jeans. She was laying there exposed in only her undergarments.

"Hand me the scalpel," Sterling ordered.

"But she isn't completely dead yet," I said, watching her blink causing tears to roll down her temples.

"That's the fun part. If they are still alive when I cut them open, then they are still alive to me once I am finished."

"You are truly one sick individual," I said, standing with my arms crossed over my chest.

"Hand me the scalpel," he ordered again, through clenched teeth.

"If you wait a few minutes she will be dead and you can do whatever you want to her, but I'm not going to allow you to torture someone right in front of me," I defied.

Faster than I could move, he was standing behind me with one arm around my waist. He reached over with his other hand and grabbed the scalpel. With the pointed edge of the blade, he pressed it into my jaw bone until it pierced my flesh then continued around my jaw line to my chin. Blood flowed down my neck and moistened my shirt.

"The next time you defy me, your entrails will be spilled out on the floor," he said, breathing in my ear.

He removed his hands from my body and walked back around the table, returning to his spot. I reached up and pressed my hand against my bleeding jaw.

He gripped the scalpel in his fist then stretched his forefinger along the back of the blade and began by making an incision from her right shoulder to her breast bone. Crimson liquid flowed from the site and rolled across her body, soaking her bra on the one side. Then, he placed the blade against her left shoulder and connected to the end of the other incision to make a 'V'. Her once mint green colored bra was now a dark cherry red.

He closed his eyes and took a few deep breaths with a smile on his face. Tears rolled from the corner of her eyes down her temples. She was still alive. Her breathing had slowed significantly since before the injection and her breaths were shallow as she gasped for air.

He opened his eyes, cut the center of her bra open and continued his incision from the two connecting points down to her pelvic bone. He had cut a perfect 'Y' shape into her torso. Blood was seeping from the incisions, covering her body.

He reached down by his side and picked up a tube. He sliced open a vein in the side of her neck and inserted the tube. He was draining her body of blood. He taped the tube to her neck so it wouldn't fall out and proceeded to pull open her torso to expose her insides.

Her eyes were vacant and no longer showed signs of life. She had passed on and I said a silent prayer for her.

He set a metal bowl up on the table next to the woman's body and began removing her organs. He reached up inside her rib cage and removed her lungs and heart. On the floor next to his feet was a bucket he dumped her intestines, stomach, liver, spleen, bladder, even her uterus into. He didn't bother cutting her organs from her body. He just pulled until each was freed then dropped them into the bucket causing a slapping noise. Each time he pulled a piece of her out, the sound it made as it sloshed into the bucket of blood, I dry heaved.

"Hand me the spray bottle," he said.

I picked up a bottle with the same color substance as what he had injected into the three others in his living quarters.

"What is this?" I asked.

"Formaldehyde, to preserve the body, with a mixture of embalming fluid, to keep the skin looking natural. I just have to make sure I continue giving her the injections and rub her down with my special formulated lotion at least twice a month so she doesn't decompose. I'm going to take care of you now, Bonnie," he spoke to the dead woman.

He sprayed down her entire body and inside her torso. I could not believe I was allowing him to make me part of this.

"Hand me the mouth guard and eye caps and before you ask the mouth guard is going to give her lips shape and help glue them together. The eye caps help keep in moisture so her eyes don't dry up and sink into the sockets," he explained as he installed those pieces.

"What's this for?" I asked referring to a can of expandable spray foam.

"That is going to fill her torso so she can keep her figure."

I felt sick to my stomach. Although, I wasn't sure if the onset of nausea was from what I had just witnessed, or blood loss.

"You should clean yourself up. Get the first aid kit from the kitchen and bandage yourself. I have work to do." He was mesmerized by the woman's body. His focus was on her as he wiped her down with a wet cloth to clean off the blood that had poured out when he cut her open.

I slowly walked toward the door. I did everything I could so as not to distract him where he would notice his mistake of letting me leave alone. Slowly opening the door, stepping into the house, I quietly closed the door behind me. I retrieved the first aid kit from the kitchen and headed into the bedroom with Gwen.

"Oh my gosh, what happened to you?" she asked, slipping out of her bindings.

"I refused to help him mutilate that girl, so he cut me," I told her, taking the first aid kit into the bathroom with me.

Gwen followed me into the lavatory and assisted me.

"You can't refuse to do what he tells you. That means you're probably going to be next. We need to figure a way out of here," she said, as she tried to help stop the bleeding.

"There is a way out, but we have to hurry. I'm surprised you didn't try to get away while we were in the back room," I said, turning toward the mirror to assess the damage.

"I tried, twice, but every time I made it to the door I thought I heard someone coming so I panicked and ran back to the room."

"Quickly, hand me some of those bandages so we can get the hell out of here."

I bandaged my face, grabbed Gwen by the arm and headed for the front door. To our surprise it was unlocked. Assuming he forgot to lock it when he was forcing the girl, he called Bonnie, into the house, we didn't really care. We were glad to have a way out.

As soon as I was able to pull the door open, we took off down the street and around the corner as fast as our legs could go. We stopped at a house and knocked on the door. No one was home. After a few more houses with the same result, we decided we were going to walk to the police station.

We stayed away from the main road and kept to the back roads with lots of covering.

We had walked a few miles, hiding in shadows every time we heard a car pass, before we realized we didn't know where we were going. We were just trying to get away

I was feeling tired and dizzy and didn't know how much further I could go. Leaning on Gwen to help me walk, she pointed out a gas station.

"Let's go in there and ask for directions," she suggested.

"I can't go in there looking like this. Someone might think I killed someone. I'm covered in blood," I told her.

"Good, then they will call the police and we will be picked up instead of having to walk the rest of the way. You don't look so good. Maybe we should get you to a hospital."

"No, forget it. We need to contact the police and have Sterling arrested."

As soon as we walked through the doors of the gas station, the attendant came out from behind the counter. She helped me into the office and sat me on a chair.

"Oh my goodness. Do you need help?" she asked, kneeling beside me.

"Yes, she needs a hospital and we need to speak to the police," Gwen told her.

"No problem." The attendant picked up the phone off the desk in the office, dialed nine-one-one and left the room.

I didn't have any energy left to argue about going to the hospital. Gwen was looking at me and I could see her mouth moving, but I couldn't hear a word she said. Just as the attendant returned to the office, I blacked out.

Twenty-Four

When I regained consciousness, I was lying in a hospital bed with heart rate patches stuck to my chest. On one side, an intravenous drip had been inserted into my left arm while the other side appeared as though it were pumping blood into my right arm. Gwen was curled up, sleeping in a chair next to the bed. I reached over and stroked her hair. She blinked her eyes rapidly until she was completely awake.

"Oh thank goodness," Gwen said, standing.

She leaned over the bed and hugged me.

"What is all this?" I asked, referring to the IV's – one in each arm.

"You lost a lot of blood. They had to give you a transfusion. That one is some kind of antibiotic to make sure you don't get an infection. Now, because your clothes were covered in blood, I had one of the police detectives take me over to the mall and she bought you a new outfit," she said, producing jeans and a designer blouse.

"Why would the police detective buy me clothes?" I asked.

"Neither one of us has any money right now. My purse was in the hotel room when I was kidnapped. I'm sure yours was too. Besides, after hearing my story she said she wanted to."

"How long do I have to be in here?"

"When the doctor came in a little while ago, he said we were just waiting for you to wake up. It has already been eight hours," Gwen informed.

"We need to get out of here and talk to the police," I said, trying to remove the heart monitor sticky patches from my chest.

"Just hold on a little longer," Gwen said, trying to hold me down on the bed while pressing the call button for the nurse.

Within seconds a nurse came through the door. I calmed down and Gwen sat in the chair she had been sleeping in. The nurse checked all the machines before speaking.

"How are you feeling, Ms. Marcum?" the nurse asked.

"I'm fine, can I go now?" I asked, trying to get up again.

"Hold on," the nurse said, putting her hands on my shoulders. "I can take out the IV, but you are going to have to wait for the doctor to release you."

"What about the blood transfusion here?" I asked, relaxing.

The nurse checked the blood bag and stopped the drip bag. She removed both needles from each arm. Grabbing a cloth and saturating it in a yellowish liquid, she rubbed iodine on the spots where the needles had been removed. The nurse also removed the heart monitor patches and replaced them with a clip on my finger. She left the room and I turned my attention back to Gwendolyn.

"How are we supposed to get to the police station?" I asked her.

"The detective is out in the waiting room. She is going to take us there."

"Hand me those clothes so I can change. This hospital gown makes me uncomfortable."

Slowly maneuvering off the bed, I pulled myself up into a standing position. Unclipping the heart monitor from my finger, I placed it on the bed. I had stood up too quickly and needed to hold onto the railing for a moment to catch my bearings. My head was swimming and my eyes were having trouble focusing.

"Anjenette, are you okay?" Gwen asked.

"I'm fine, just give me a minute. I stood up a little too fast. It's all coming back to me now," I said, as my focus returned and my head cleared.

I took the clothes from Gwen and headed into the bathroom. When I started to close the door, Gwen protested.

"Leave it open, in case something happens and I have to go in there to help you," Gwen said.

"Okay, but only a crack. The second the door to this room opens though, it will be latched shut," I told her.

I left the door cracked open, then examined myself in the mirror. I had a bruise on the opposite side of my face from the cut along my jawline. I lifted my head slightly to examine the damage Sterling had caused. A few stitches from the hospital and I knew I was going to have a scar for life. My arm was wrapped with a bandage so I didn't disturb it to see what the doctors had done with Mateo's handiwork.

I swapped the hospital gown for the clothes Gwen had given me. I took one more look in the mirror, then returned to the bed.

"Are you feeling okay?" Gwen asked, as I lay down on the bed.

"I'm fine. I just want to leave," I said.

I thought about the fact that two different people had tried to kill me hours apart. Sterling implied he had killed Mateo, but I had an uneasy feeling he would come back to haunt me.

A couple hours later, we were in the detective's car heading for the police station.

"Ms. Marcum, do you think you are feeling well enough to answer some questions?" the detective asked, as we arrived at the station.

"No problem, as long as we can get this guy behind bars," I said, staring out the window.

The detective pulled up in front of the building, got out of the car and came around to the passenger side to let us out of the back seat. She assisted me into a standing position.

"I'm going to go park the car. Wait for me inside."

Gwen and I headed up to the door. She pulled it open and held it for me. We stepped into a waiting area where Doreen and Francine occupied two of the eight chairs along the wall. They looked up when we came in. Both of their expressions changed from sorrow, to shock, to elation within seconds.

"Gwendolyn, my baby girl. You're alive," Doreen shouted, as she embraced her daughter.

"Anjenette, what happened?" Francine inquired about my face.

"Long story, I'll tell you about later," I said.

"How did you get here?" Doreen asked, her arms still wrapped around Gwen.

"A police detective brought us from the hospital," Gwen answered.

"The hospital?" Are you okay?" Doreen asked, inspecting every inch of Gwen.

"I'm fine. We were there because of what he did to Anjie. Look at her face," Gwen explained.

Doreen kept her eyes locked on Gwen, never acknowledging that I was even there. The detective interrupted our reunion when she came through the door.

"Come on, ladies. We need to get your statements of what happened," the detective said, as she passed her gun to a uniformed officer who was sitting in a box encased in glass. A small square was cut out, twelve inches by twelve inches, with a twelve inch by five inch size counter piece fit into the bottom of the square for the officers to leave their fire arms before entering the station.

There was a buzzing sound before the detective reached out and grabbed the inner door. She pulled it open and the buzzing stopped. Francine and Doreen started to follow us in, but the detective stopped them.

"You two are going to have to wait out here. You can see them as soon as I am done interviewing them," the detective said.

"I'm not letting my daughter out of my sight again. She has been missing for four months, I begin thinking the worst has happened, when all of a sudden she is brought back into my life and you want to take her away again. I don't think so," Doreen argued, grabbing Gwen's arm.

The detective rolled her eyes. "Ugh, fine." She turns toward Francine. "I suppose this is your sister and now I'm ripping her from your life again as well?"

The confrontational tone in the detective's voice made Francine nervous. She couldn't speak. She sat down on the floor, put on her headphones and hugged her knees as she rocked back and forth.

I crouched down beside Francine and gently touched her knee. She pulled off the headphones and looked me in the eyes.

"She yelled at me," Francine said, in a childlike voice.

"I know, it's okay. Come on, you can come too." I assisted Francine to her feet, then turned my focus on the detective. "She has Asperger's, detective. I am her comforter."

"I guess we're all going then," the detective said, with a heavy sigh.

She led us to a desk where she sat behind it while Gwen and I sat in the two chairs in front. Doreen stood behind Gwen as Francine stood behind me.

"Ms. Welsh, I was able to get your statement back at the hospital, but would you like to tell your story again so your mother will know?" the detective asked.

"Not right now. I think I am going to wait until we are home so I can tell my father at the same time," Gwen decided.

"Okay, Ms. Marcum, how about you? What can you tell me about what happened to you?"

"Is there a way you could just get me a pen and paper and I could write it down. I don't think I am ready to say all of this out loud yet," I responded.

"Sure thing. Easier on me anyway," the detective commented, as she retrieved a legal pad and a blue gel pen from her desk drawer.

The detective left as I began writing. I started with the encounter with Mateo, then worked my way up to Sterling. I even mentioned what he tried to make me do, yet I refused, explaining the mark on my face.

The detective returned just as I was finishing my statement. I handed her the note pad and she looked over what I had written.

"Alright, we will investigate this person and let you know," the detective said.

"Investigate what?" Francine sounded enraged. "They have already implicated a suspect."

"We will do surveillance on the house, gather up a little more information on the guy, then we will let you know. Thank you for coming in." She stood from behind the desk and walked away.

"Something fishy is going on here. We need to get home and talk to the FBI agents on the case there," Doreen said, looking around the station.

Twenty-Five

The four of us headed for the door and exited the police station. Gwen and I followed Doreen and Francine as they led the way to a rental car.

"Where did you get this?" I asked, as we piled into the vehicle.

Doreen stuck the key into the ignition and turned over the engine. "I got it from a car rental place a couple of blocks from the hotel. The nice young lady behind the counter that wrapped up your arm had called the cops. We waited with an officer for forty-five minutes before going up to the room. You were gone, so we told the officer what had happened and about Mateo. We followed the officer back down to the lobby where the conference was taking place and watched him arrest Mateo."

She shifted the car into reverse and backed out of the parking space. Driving approximately fifty miles an hour, Doreen guided the car down the street heading for the freeway toward the hotel. I knew I would have to explain to my boss why I missed the rest of the conference, but I just wanted to go home.

"That still doesn't explain the car," I said.

"The officer gave us one of his cards and told us to meet him at the station. So, we went to the rental car place and ended up at the station," Doreen said.

"Is Mateo being charged with my abduction?" I asked.

"No charges were filed. Because you were gone, the officer said there wasn't any evidence of what we were claiming, so they let him go. The officer said you could have run off on your own to hide from him," Francine informed.

We made it back to the room and packed our luggage. Once we had all the bags ready to go, we headed down to the lobby to check out.

"Anjie, take Francine and Gwen and go over to check out of the hotel. When you are finished, call a cab to come pick us up to take us to the airport. I'm going to return the rental car and I should be back before the cab gets here," Doreen instructed.

"Are you sure you should go by yourself? What if Sterling comes back and takes you as a way to lore Gwen?" I asked.

"That asshole won't know who he's messing with if he tries anything with me," Doreen said, acting as if she were tough.

"Be careful," Gwen said, hugging her mother.

"I'll be on alert. Don't worry." Doreen touched her daughter's face in a loving way.

She headed back toward the elevators to ride down to the parking garage. Gwen, Francine and I headed over to the front counter.

"We need to check out please," I told the clerk, setting the key cards down on the counter.

It wasn't the same helpful clerk as before. This one was much less aware of her surrounding nor did she act like she cared.

"No problem. How was your stay?" she asked in a sullen tone, as she printed the bill.

We all looked at each other, but never said a word.

"That's good," she commented, telling us she wasn't really listening anyway.

"Here, use this card to pay for the hotel. I'm going to call the cab company," I told Francine, handing her my corporate card.

Linking my arm with Gwen, I led her over near the door and called for a cab while we watched for Doreen. As I ended the call, Francine stepped up next to me and joined us.

We grabbed the suitcases and stepped through the doors to the outside just as Doreen came walking around the corner. We set down the luggage in front of a bench to wait for the cab.

"Thank goodness. What took you so long?" Gwen asked, embracing her mother.

"I've only been gone twenty minutes," Doreen responded.

The cab pulled up to the curb in front of us and the driver got out helping put our bags in the trunk. Doreen rode in the front passenger seat while Gwen, Francine and I crammed in the back. We decided it was best not to discuss our situation in front of strangers, so the entire ride to the airport was silent.

He stopped next to the curb at the airport and popped the trunk open for us. This time he didn't get out. As Doreen paid the driver, I retrieved Francine's bag first and handed it to her, then Doreen's; passing it over to her. My bag was last and as soon as I closed the trunk the cab driver drove off as fast as he could.

"I guess he didn't like the fact that we didn't engage in conversation," Francine analyzed.

"I guess not. Must be all the entertainment he gets on a daily basis is whatever the people in his cab say," I bantered.

We stepped inside the airport and got in line for tickets. It had only been two days since we had arrived. I was going to transfer our tickets, which were for the next night, and purchase one extra for Gwen.

Luckily, it was late enough that hardly anyone was flying out so the lady at the ticket counter said it was no problem to swap them.

"Also, I can down grade your three first class tickets to coach and you can use the extra money for the fourth with no out of pocket expense," the lady told me.

"Hang on," I told her.

I motioned for Francine to come over. She walked up to me and I could tell she was creating her private bubble. I explained the situation to her.

"How many people are on the flight?" she asked, looking nervous.

I looked at the lady behind the ticket counter. She drummed her fingers on the keyboard, then gave me a number.

"Between twenty and forty, but the plane will hold one hundred and fifty people so it will be like it is almost empty," I relayed the information to Francine.

"Well, okay. Hopefully a stranger doesn't want to talk to me," she said.

"It's an hour and a half flight in the middle of the night. Most people will be sleeping," I said, dismissing her.

Francine returned to her spot next to Gwen and Doreen. I went ahead and agreed to the down grade.

"Can you make sure we have four seats together?" I asked.

"Absolutely," she said, as she typed our information into the computer and produced our tickets.

I called my mother while we waited to board the plane and asked her to pick us up at the airport when we landed. I didn't tell her what happened or that we had found Gwen.

"Coming home a little early?" she asked.

"Just a little. We had some complications I will tell you about when we get home," I explained and hung up before she could ask any more questions.

"My mother said she would be there to pick us up when the plane lands," I informed the others.

"Did it seem odd to anyone else how the detective just blew us off like that? It was almost as if she thought we were lying," Gwen said.

"But it wasn't until she walked away from the desk to allow Anjie to write down her account of events," Doreen mentioned.

"That's true. She seemed really sympathetic to me, but changed her tune after she read what Anjenette wrote down," Gwen revealed.

"What did you say?" Doreen accused.

"I wrote down exactly what happened," I said.

"Did you make it all about you?" Doreen asked.

"I only wrote down what happened to me since Gwen already told her what happened to her," I explained.

"Like you said, Mom, it wasn't until she walked away. She was nice, then when she came back, she was singing a different tune. Maybe she had talked to someone who changed her mind," Gwen said.

"Maybe the name Edward Nilsen triggered something," I told them.

"Maybe they searched Sterling Bigum, found out he no longer exists and assumed y'all were lying," Francine suggested.

I was relieved when our flight number was called for boarding. We picked up our luggage and headed toward the gate. The attendant checked our tickets and waved us into the tunnel toward the plane. We found our seats and stuffed our bags into the overhead compartment. We were able to get the four middle seats right next to each other.

"There has to be more houses with rotting corpses inside that have yet to be found. Agent Herring only told us about two, Theodore Ramirez and Dennis Ridgeway. Sterling confessed to me there were six," I said, as soon as we sat down. I pulled a small note pad and pen from my purse.

"What name was he going by when he abducted you?" Doreen asked Gwen.

"He said his name was John Bernardo," Gwen answered.

"He told me his name was Edward Nilsen," I said, as I listed the names.

"I know what he is doing," Francine chimed in.

"What are you talking about?" Doreen inquired.

"Well, he started, that we know of, as Theodore Ramirez, but Anjie said his neighbors called him Ted. Like Ted Bundy. His last name Ramirez, like Richard Ramirez. Ted Bundy claimed over thirty lives where the police believe it could be as high as one hundred and Richard Ramirez murdered at least fourteen," Francine informed.

"They're both serial killers. So," Doreen said, condescendingly.

"The second house, Dennis Ridgeway. Dennis Radar was BTK and Gary Ridgeway was the Green River Killer," Francine continued.

The plane began to taxi down the runway and we realized we missed the safety announcement. We each checked and made sure we had our seat belts on, then leaned back and waited for the plane to ascend.

"Are you sure he didn't just make up these names?" Doreen said, once the plane leveled out in the air.

"John Bernardo is John Wayne Gacy and Paul Bernardo. John Wayne Gacy was the guy who dressed up like a clown for neighborhood get togethers and kids birthday parties. He used to pick up young gay men, then kill them and bury them in the crawl space under his house. Paul Bernardo would kidnap teenage girls and hold them hostage in his house for days and rape them repeatedly, then kill them while his wife videotaped it.

"This last one, Edward Nilsen. It is almost poetic. Edward or Ed Gein only technically killed two women. He was a grave robber. He would remove their skin so he could wear pieces of them. He also had several furniture items throughout his house made of human flesh and bones. He is the reason we have Leather Face from Texas Chainsaw Massacre, Norman Bates from Psycho and Buffalo Bill from Silence of the Lambs.

"Last, but not least, Dennis Nilsen. He was a gay man who just wanted a friend. He would bring someone home, then kill them when they tried to leave. It almost seems fitting for Sterling to use Nilsen's name. The only difference is that Dennis Nilsen would dismember his victims and hide them under the floor before disposing of the bodies because they started to smell. He never tried to preserve his victims like Sterling," Francine explained.

"That makes sense," I said. "A serial killer using serial killer names."

"Someone has to stop him, but how many more people have to die before he is caught?" Gwen asked.

"I don't know, but hopefully the FBI and police back home will help us catch this son of a bitch and soon," I said.

"Attention passengers, we will be making our final decent. Please make sure your seat backs and tray tables are in the upright and locked position. You'll notice the pilot has turned on the fasten seatbelt sign. Please remain seated with your seatbelt securely fastened until we come to a complete stop and the pilot has turned off the seatbelt sign. On behalf of all of us at Blue Bird Airlines, we hope you have enjoyed your flight and you use us for all your travel needs," the flight attendant announced.

We complied with the instructions and sat quietly until we were able to unbuckle our seatbelts. Doreen stood and opened the overhead compartment. She retrieved the luggage and closed the compartment.

"Where are we supposed to meet your mother?" Doreen asked, as we exited the airplane.

"She will be waiting for us by the baggage claim carousel," I answered.

As soon as we had made it out of the tunnel and into the open airport, I walked as fast as I could to my mother. Francine, Gwen and Doreen tried to keep up as best they could.

My mother noticed Gwen and her face lit up.

"How did you find her?" my mother asked. Then noticing my bandages, "What happened to you?" her tone shifting to concern.

"He got me too. We managed to escape," I kept my answer short.

"He cut you up," my mother said, acknowledging my face and arm.

"Actually, Sterling only messed up my face," I told her, as we began walking through the airport toward the car.

"Then what happened to your arm?"

"Mateo showed up at the conference," Francine told her.

"The crazy guy who broke into your house?" my mother ranted.

I nodded as we approached the vehicle. I climbed into the front passenger seat next to my mother as the others piled in the back. My mother started the engine.

"Did Sterling harm you in any way, Gwendolyn?" my mother inquired.

"Hold on now. She hasn't told *me* anything yet," Doreen complained.

"Laird is at the house with Wade. We can all hear the full story when we get there," my mother said.

"Laird came over in the middle of the night? Why?" Doreen wondered.

"I could tell by the tone in her voice that Anjenette had something important to tell us, but I wasn't sure what it was. Just in case it had something to do with Gwen, I called Laird to come over," my mother explained.

I looked back at Francine and she appeared to be nervous. I decided she had had enough excitement for the day.

"Mom, you think you could drop Francine off at her apartment on the way?" I suggested.

"Sure, no problem. Are you doing okay back there Francie?" my mother asked.

"Yes ma'am, for now," Francine responded, her voice was shaky.

She mouthed 'Thank you' to me and I nodded before turning back around to stare out the windshield.

Twenty-Six

When we arrived at my parents' house, my father and Laird were sitting in the living room, waiting. As soon as he noticed Gwen, Laird jumped out of his seat and embraced his daughter. My father noticed my injuries and stood up as well.

"Anjie sweetie, what happened?" my father asked, cradling my arm with his hands.

"How much time do you have?" I asked.

"All the time in the world for you," he said, wrapping his arms around me.

Laird couldn't speak. I could see him trying to choke back his tears. He had no reason to be strong anymore; his baby girl had come home.

"Let's have a seat. I want to know what happened," Doreen said, trying to break up the reunion.

We all sat down and Gwen began. I kept thinking about that poor girl. I felt so ashamed I had helped Sterling mutilate that woman. What made me feel even worse was that I wasn't even sure what her real name was.

I decided that I should describe everything I could remember about her to Agent Herring. The FBI had resources at their disposal to compare the description I give to an actual missing person.

"Anjenette?" Gwen said, touching my shoulder.

"I'm sorry, what did you say?" I asked, realizing I hadn't been paying attention.

"I stopped at the part where you came into the bedroom with me. I figured you could fill in the blanks," Gwen said.

"Oh, okay," I said.

I started thinking about the woman Darla, Sterling's servant. Where did he find her? What did she do to him that made him want to kill her? Then I thought about Tom and Jerry. Was that just an odd coincidence, or did he give them those names?

Sterling had a childish quality about him when he referred to them. I could only assume that was why he chose those names.

"Anjenette? Are you okay?" Gwen asked, pulling me out of my thought, again.

"We need to go talk to Agent Herring," I said, standing.

"We should all go," Doreen said.

"I think Gwen and I should go alone," I suggested, helping Gwen into a standing position.

"No way am I letting her out of my sight again. I'm going with you." Doreen stood and wrapped her arms around Gwen.

"Doreen, we need to be grown up about this," I told her.

"What, you don't feel grown up if you go with your mommy?" Doreen mocked.

"Really Doreen, is that absolutely necessary?" my mother asked.

"You didn't see the way she treated me at the airport before we left," Doreen complained.

"So in your defense, you retaliate? You are a grown woman, for crying out loud. Why don't you act like one," my mother scolded.

"Look, let's get back on subject. I'm not going to debate this. Either I go with you, or Gwen stays here," Doreen said, crossing her arms over her chest.

"I can't believe you're acting like this," I said, walking off into the kitchen.

My mother and Gwen followed me. I slammed the palm of my hands against the counter.

"Why does she always have to be that way?" I asked, slapping the counter a few more times.

"Anjie, you have to realize, she lost her daughter for four months and she sees this as you trying to take her away again," my mother explained.

"So she decides to act like Sterling?" I griped.

"Anjie, really?" my mother reprimanded.

"I lost my best friend," I said, walking over to Gwen. "The only difference was I never stopped looking for her. Doreen was the one who was waiting for the phone call saying Gwen's body had been found. I don't think she has the right to go with us."

"I don't think she gave up thinking Gwen was alive; I think she was just trying to get closure before she got the call. That way she could be prepared for it. Whether you think she has the right or not, she is her mother. You have to understand, if I was in her position, I wouldn't want to let *you* out of my sight," my mother said.

"Think about it this way, you arguing with her is not making the situation any better," Gwen told me.

"Alright, but how can I convince her not to go?" I asked.

"That's not going to happen and why does it matter anyway?" Gwen said.

"We have to do something," I said. "We have to get him."

"What do you mean get him?" Gwen asked.

I looked at my mother and could see her thought process working. She nodded at me as though she understood what I was thinking.

"I may have a plan," my mother began. "I know what you're going to do and I know that Doreen would not approve."

"Anjie, what is she talking about? What are you going to do?" Gwen asked.

"I know we can get Sterling for what he has done. If Doreen comes along, we won't be able to…" I trailed off.

"What are you planning?" Gwen shifted her focus to my mother, "and why are you helping her? She was abducted and injured by the same maniac."

"Because I know she will include me," my mother said, smiling.

"It's best if you don't know until the last minute," I said, heading back toward the living room with my mother and Gwen close behind.

"Look, I understand you are trying to be a grown up, but no matter how old children become, they will always be their parents' babies. There is a strong need to always protect our children and hopefully someday you will understand that," Doreen explained, as we approached.

"I get your need to protect your child, what I don't get is your refusal to let go," I said.

"Why don't we all go? Laird and Wade, you can go in one car and the rest of us can go in my car. On the way, Anjie, you can tell us what happened to you," my mother suggested.

She had something on her mind and she was willing to help me while pacifying Doreen. I wasn't sure yet what she was thinking, but I knew my mother and how much she enjoyed trying to one up Doreen on the 'Best Mother in the World' scale.

"Fine, I think I can compromise on that. See Anjenette, your mother agrees with me. She wants to keep you safe as well," Doreen said.

I looked at my mother and she was grinning from ear to ear. I didn't know what she had planned, but it had to be something good. I knew it would piss off Doreen, so I let her continue to plot. She handed me the keys to her sedan so I could drive.

"So, we don't get to hear the story?" my father said.

"Maybe later dad," I said, kissing him on the cheek.

"Fine, but I want to know whose ass I am supposed to kick for messing up my beautiful daughter's face," my father said, stroking my cheek.

We left the house and approached the vehicles. Laird and my father were in the Welsh's car, while the rest of us piled into my mother's car. We headed down the street toward the police station and I recalled the events that led up to the rescue and escape of Gwen, while my mother and Doreen listened intently.

Twenty-Seven

Since Herring and the other FBI agents had found the Dennis Ridgeway house in the next county past Sundaisy, we had to drive an extra hour. They had relocated to the Terrybell police station.

When we arrived they appeared to be on their way out. Herring stopped when she spotted us. Agents Jarvis and Fleck continued past us to the government issued Crown Victoria.

"Agent Herring, this is Gwendolyn Welsh," I introduced.

Agent Herring's facial expression changed as she stared at Gwen. It was almost as though she had seen a ghost.

"So, *this* is Gwendolyn Welsh? Well then, we have made a horrible mistake. I am so glad we waited to contact you all." Herring looked embarrassed as her cheeks tinted a rosy color.

"What happened?" I asked.

"Why don't you all come inside? Let me inform Jarvis and Fleck of the situation and we can talk," Herring said, leading us inside.

We sat down and waited for her while she went out to the car to bring the other two agents back in. The Terrybell police station was smaller than the one out in Sundaisy. It looked like our group of six was larger than their entire police force.

"Anjie, could you help me find the bathroom. That long drive has my bladder screaming for relief," my mother said, uncensored.

"Great, I'll go with you. I could use a little freshening up," Doreen said, joining us.

"NO," my mother said, a little too loud. "I have a shy bladder. I can't go if I know there is a group."

"Fine, I'll wait," Doreen said, confused.

"We'll be right back," I said, leading my mother away from the others.

The bathrooms were hidden back in a corner of the station. Once we were inside, my mother checked the two stalls, which were empty.

"Okay, here's the plan. I gave you the keys to my car so it wouldn't look suspicious when you storm off later if I had to hand them to you. You need to get the address to that house. Find a reason to argue with Doreen. I know you can do that. Grab Gwen and head toward the car. Text me the address and we can meet you there," my mother laid it all out.

"Why do y'all need to be there?" I asked.

"Safety, in case something happens we will be there to call for help."

"Fine, but don't let Doreen talk Gwen out of confronting her demon," I said, as the bathroom door opened.

"What are you two doing in here?" Doreen asked, coming through the door. "The agents are waiting."

She motioned for us to follow her and we all headed back to the seating area.

Herring, Jarvis and Fleck were standing, waiting for the three of us to join them. We scrambled to try and find enough chairs for us all to sit. Once we were all seated, Jarvis asked about Gwen.

"Who's she?" Jarvis asked.

"This is Gwendolyn Welsh," Herring answered, with an awkward tone.

"Then who is the…" Fleck started.

"Okay, well," Herring interrupted. "We were on our way out to investigate a third house with about a dozen bodies inside and an extensive graveyard in the back, just like the others. One of the ladies who was found in the bedroom red flagged as Gwendolyn Welsh. So, the Marshland police department called us to come take a look. Once we confirmed it, you would have been notified."

"Let me guess, the house was registered under the name John Bernardo?" Gwen asked. "I was there."

"That's right," Herring agreed. "If you were there, we need you to come with us to identify the body if you don't mind."

"I may know exactly who she is, or at least who he told me she was," Gwen revealed.

"We will need to inform the coroner of this new found information," Fleck stated.

We all stood and headed back out to the vehicles to drive to the Marshland police department. It was another two hour drive, but at least it was closer to the Edward Nilsen house.

"He doesn't seem to travel far, does he?" Doreen said, after a few minutes into the drive in order to break the silence.

"I guess not. The only problem is there are still two houses unaccounted for with rotting corpses. How is it he can do this for so long without anyone noticing?" my mother commented.

"My question is, how many people a day is he abducting and killing? Not only that, but how long has he been doing this, that there are dozens of bodies being found?" I wondered out loud.

"We still have a little over an hour to go, let's do the math," Doreen suggested.

"There were fifteen bodies *inside* the Theodore Ramirez house. I believe they found about twice that outside buried in the backyard. Assuming he only lived in that house for a month, with forty five bodies in a thirty day month, he had to be abducting at least one person a day with some days two," I figured.

"So we can assume that Monday through Friday were his single abduction days, while his weekends were reserved for double abductions," Doreen said.

"That is only to say the month had four weekends," my mother responded.

"Could we please stop talking about this?" Gwen asked, shuttering.

"I'm sorry, honey. If it is making you uncomfortable, we'll stop," I told her.

"We are just trying to understand how he was able to kill that many people," Doreen said.

"Mother, please stop. I don't want to understand, I just want to get this fucker and move on with my life," Gwen chastised.

The remaining twenty minute drive was silent. I watched my mother and Doreen in the rearview mirror. My mother smirked and Doreen just stared out the window. I peered over at Gwen. She wasn't the same timid girl she was six months prior to that point. She had turned into a strong willed woman. I knew then that she would be able to confront Sterling without cowering in fear.

When we arrived at the Marshland police department there wasn't a lot of activity outside, but inside was a different story. Police were talking to grieving family members of those found in the John Bernardo house.

"I'm gonna kill that son of a bitch that did this to my daughter," one man shouted as he left the station.

"They just started informing the families of missing people that their loved ones had been found," Jarvis said.

"Did they call everyone in the town to come out? Some of these people appear relieved while others appear distraught," Laird said.

"Not just those in town. Some of these people came from neighboring counties. If their missing loved one matched any close description of the deceased, they were called in to identify the body. Some have had two or three and sometimes five families positively identify them as their missing loved one. Hi, I'm Detective Roads. I'm the lead investigator on this case," a gentleman dressed in an incredibly wrinkled brown suit informed us.

"Nice to meet you, Detective. I'm Agent Jarvis. This is Agent Fleck and Agent Herring with the FBI."

"Glad to have you with us assisting with the investigation. The Welsh girl is back this way," the detective said, leading us to the back of the police station. "Is this her family?"

"Actually, in that case we have some good news," Herring said.

Detective Roads stopped walking and turned around. "What do you mean good news?"

"Is there a room we can all go to and talk privately?" Herring asked.

"Yeah, sure," Roads said, leading us into an interrogation room.

He instructed all of us, except the FBI agents to grab a chair just before entering the room. There was a rectangular table in the center of the room with two chairs on one side and one chair across the table from the pair. We placed our chairs around the table and sat down.

"Detective Roads, *this* is Gwendolyn Welsh," Herring said, introducing Gwen as we sat.

He looked at Gwen as though it were the first time he noticed her. He stood up and walked over, standing behind my friend. She sat very still as the detective examined her.

"Wow, it really is uncanny," Roads said.

"What is detective?" Doreen asked.

"The woman we found. She could be her twin," he said.

"Now I'm sure I know who it is. He told me her name was Gwyneth," Gwen said.

"There has to be some differences," Laird spoke up.

"Oh no, this woman could be her doppelganger," Roads said.

"Can I see her?" Gwen asked.

"Why would you want to see her?" Doreen asked.

"She was the only person I had to talk to every night after he had raped me. As strange as it seems, I would really like to say good bye," Gwen said with tears rolling down her cheeks.

"Of course you can. Would you like Anjenette to come with you?" Herring asked.

"I would appreciate it," Gwen answered.

"I'm going too," Doreen announced.

"Please just stay here. I am going to be with Anjenette, Agent Herring and Detective Roads. Stay here with the other two agents," Gwen said.

Laird reached up and grabbed Doreen's hand. She looked down at her spouse and lowered herself back into the chair. A look of sadness and disappointment took over her expression.

The police station was situated on a large island like property which was surrounded by roads on all four sides. It only took up a small amount of the property, while a hospital was the primary building. Herring and Roads led us out the back of the station toward a separate building which was not visible from any of the streets. It was encased in grey brick with a grey painted door that faced the station. A sign above the door read 'Morgue'. It was practically in the police station's back yard only separating the two buildings with a parking lot.

On the side of the grey structure was a tunnel like hallway which lined the center of the property and attached to one of the back entrances to the hospital.

"What is that for?" I enquired.

"It is the route the coroner takes when someone in the hospital dies. The body is discreetly removed from the room in which they passed on and wheeled through the hallway into the morgue without anyone noticing. Best part about having it there is, when the hospital calls about a possible domestic violence situation, we can sneak in through the back and the abuser never even knows we have entered the building," Roads said, with a sort of giddy tone in his voice.

Roads opened the door to the morgue and the four of us stepped into a small vestibule with another door to the left and a receptionist counter about ten feet across from the main door. Roads stepped up to the front counter.

"Hello Agnes. We need to speak to Frank," he said.

The smell of formaldehyde and death invaded my nasal cavity as we stood waiting for the eighty something year old woman to figure out how to let us in. She fumbled around as though she were looking for something.

"Not many people come in for a visit. I can never remember where the button to unlock the door is," Agnes said, as she felt around on the underside of the desk. "There it is."

Finally, the inner door buzzed and Roads pulled it open. Gwen reached over and held my hand as we stepped through the door into a hallway. Within a few feet we stopped in front of a room with one inner wall all windows so we could observe from the hallway. The other three walls where stainless steel with several body drawers in each wall. The man inside was examining a body.

"I'm going to go in and talk to him for a moment. Agent, would you like to accompany me, seeing as how you know more about this case than I do?" Roads asked Herring.

"Sure. The two of you wait here while we go in to inform the coroner of the mistake," Herring said.

Gwen continued to hold my hand as Roads and Herring entered the room. We watched as the man Roads called Frank draped a sheet over the body he was examining. As Herring spoke, Frank appeared confused and stepped over to one of the three feet by three feet drawers in the far wall. He opened the small freezer like door and pulled the body out. A white sheet was draped over the body to which Frank folded over to the shoulders to expose her face.

Herring gestured toward the two of us on the other side of the window. Frank looked in our direction and his face drained of all color. It was as though he were facing his ultimate nightmare. He looked back and forth between Gwen and the girl lying on the table.

Frank moved toward the door, but kept his eyes locked on Gwen as though if he were to look away she would disappear.

He opened the door and only looked away for that split second it took him to pass his gaze from the inside of the room to out into the hallway.

Twenty-Eight

"**P**lease, come in," Frank said, motioning us through the door. He did a backward wave like an infant who was just learning the motion.

He led us over to where Gwyneth was lying. Gwendolyn immediately had tears pooling in her lower lids. The smell in the room was stronger, more pungent. The body itself had its own strong odor and the skin was almost grey in color.

Gwen stroked the hair of the dead girl and cried.

"I'm so sorry this happened to you. I'm sorry you were dragged into this whole mess. This is all my fault," Gwen spoke to Gwyneth.

"This is not your fault," I tried to reassure her.

"It is my fault. I did this to her," Gwen confessed.

"No Gwen, Sterling did this to her," I said.

"I helped him. And I kept her. He told me exactly what to do to keep her from decomposing," Gwen said. "And I did it."

"I found several different injection sights in the iliac and femoral arteries as well as the subclavian and axillary vessels and common carotids. He did his research and knew exactly where the formaldehyde/glutaraldehyde mixture was to be injected in order to keep her preserved," Frank informed.

"He marked each spot where she needed to be injected and left me with a bottle of some kind of lotion that needed to be rubbed over her entire body to ensure thorough saturation of body tissues. I'm no better than he is. I kept her this way for the same reason he kept all those other people. I just wanted someone to talk to."

"This is not your fault. You did not go out and choose this girl for this purpose," I told her.

"I know that, but I did this to her. She was alive before I injected her with all those chemicals. I apologized to her every day, but that was after she was dead. She didn't know how truly sorry I was for what I had done to her." Gwen had tears streaking her make-up down her face.

I grabbed her and embraced her. "Listen to me. This is in no way your fault. Do not blame yourself."

"Okay, now that we have a positive identification we can go back and contact her family," Roads said, trying to lead us out.

"I'm sorry detective, but I don't think Gwyneth is her real name," I commented, pulling away from Gwen's grasp.

"I understand that, but now that we know this is not her," he said, referring to Gwen. "We can sort through more missing person photos and contact her real family."

"If she came in contact with any form of formaldehyde, that includes the lotion, she needs to have her blood checked at a hospital," Frank suggested, as he pushed Gwyneth back into the wall.

"Why, what could happen?" Gwen asked.

"The chemical can seep into your skin and enter your blood stream causing blood cancer. I wouldn't be surprised if you had blistering on your hands from it."

Gwen looked down at her hands and noticed all the identifying marks of her fingers and the palms of her hands were gone. It was as though Sterling knew the chemical would burn off any ridge detail of her finger prints so she couldn't be properly identified. Gwen dropped to her knees.

"What do I do? How do I take it back?" Gwen cried.

"Go get checked out and the doctors will tell you what to do," Frank said, helping her to her feet.

We headed out, back to the station. The fresh air outside had a clean smell to it compared to the inside of the morgue. The stench inside was beginning to weigh me down and the fresh air outside along with the openness seemed to lift the weight off me.

We were led through the back door of the police station and into a cafeteria of sorts. There were three round tables with four chairs each placed strategically in the center of the room. Three separate vending machines were lined up along the back wall. One held assorted bottled beverages; one held snacks and the last was sandwiches. There was counter space and a sink along the same wall with the door.

My parents, along with Doreen and Laird, were sitting at one of the tables waiting for us. We moved a couple of chairs from the other tables to join them.

"Please wait here," Herring instructed, before closing the door.

"Gwen, have you been crying?" Doreen asked.

"Seeing her again just brought back the horror of what we had been through," Gwen said, rubbing her face.

She looked at me and mouthed 'Don't', which told me she didn't want her mother to know about her hands or the possibility of any kind of cancer. I obliged and sat down without saying a word about it.

"It's over now. You're home and safe," Doreen attempted encouragement.

"I don't know how safe I really am. Sterling is still out there and who knows what he is planning next," Gwen said.

"I agree. If he was plotting for all those years he was in prison, who's to say he's not thinking about her now," my mother told Doreen.

Doreen's face contorted as she readied herself with a comeback. She was content with thinking her daughter was safe, then my mother chimed in with negativity.

I was relieved when Herring returned with Agent Fleck, Agent Jarvis and Detective Roads in tow before Doreen began her rant. They positioned four chairs at the table closest to Gwen.

"Why do you think he spared you from death compared to the other victims?" Jarvis began.

"I can hardly say spared, agent," Gwen said, looking down at her hands.

"Why does that matter?" I asked.

Gwen placed a calming hand on my arm. "He said he wanted a part of me to live on, so he raped me until I became pregnant."

"There wasn't any signs of sexual assault on any of the other victims, why just you?" Jarvis inquired.

"Are you calling her a liar?" I yelled.

"Calm down Ms. Marcum. We are just trying to understand why she was the only one who was assaulted and left alive," Herring assured.

"She is technically his first victim. He has held her hostage before. She is the reason he went to jail. It is possible he is obsessed with her," I replied.

"It is also possible he wanted me to have a slow painful death as well," Gwen said, holding out her hands. "No need to inject me with a paralytic drug if I was already dying."

"It can also cause birth defects. You may need to have the baby checked out as well," Herring spoke with a calming tone.

"I'm sure she doesn't plan on keeping the spawn of Satan. She is probably planning to give it up for adoption anyway so she doesn't care what it looks like," I said.

"Anjenette, if you want to help Gwen with her independence, why don't you let her answer the questions," my mother said, in a calm tone.

I stood from the table and walked over to the counter area. I peered through the window in front of me which looked out into the station. I listened as they continued to question Gwen.

"We will have to travel to where Edward Nilsen is and speak to the police there before we can arrest him. According to our research, Nilsen is still an active alias. The other names have come up empty, other than matching the homes that have been found," Jarvis informed.

"Since you have eye witnesses to the heinousness that is Edward Nilsen, can't you just get a warrant and storm his house?" Doreen asked.

"Unfortunately, no. The local police have to be informed and conduct a thorough investigation before storming into someone's home," Herring said. "If he gets the right defense attorney he can claim the search was unfounded and his rights were infringed upon. In that case the grand jury can only acquit him and he ends up back out on the streets."

"Luckily, we were able to obtain an address considering the description you gave us of the house," Jarvis said, irritated.

I walked over and stood behind the federal agents as Fleck opened the file sitting in front of him.

"The house appears to have windows on the outside, but once you get inside there aren't any," Fleck read.

I jotted down the address from the file on the palm of my hand.

"Neither one of us got a good look at the house as we were being dragged in or when we were running away from it. What more did you want? At least now you know he won't see you coming," Gwen told Jarvis.

"We will inform the police where the Nilsen house is and help them set up surveillance on the home. Once they have the evidence needed, they can decide when and how to proceed with an arrest," Jarvis said.

"I thought the FBI trumped local police and could take down a suspect and question them without reason?" my father finally spoke.

"Technically yes, we can go in and say we are above them and we are going to apprehend a suspected killer. Unfortunately, Jarvis here knows all too well how bad that approach can go," Herring said.

"Fine, you watch and we'll take action," I said, heading for the door.

"If you interfere with this investigation, we will arrest *you*," Jarvis said, as he stood.

I walked back over to the table and stood next to Gwen.

"We don't plan to interfere detective, we plan to take over." I grabbed Gwen's hand and we started to leave.

"Please, just let us handle this," Herring said.

"I can let you handle the arrest, but we are going to handle the capture."

Gwen and I left the room and started for the car. My parents along with Laird and Doreen stayed behind to continue talking with the agents. Gwen and I sat in my mother's car in front of the police station. The sun was emerging from the horizon, emitting an orange glow.

"We need to get going," I said, as I started the car.

"Where are we going?" Gwen asked.

"We are going to get Sterling on our own," I replied, pulling out of the parking space.

"How are we going to find the house? We aren't even too sure where he lives," Gwen said, as I merged onto the interstate.

"I got the address off the file when Fleck opened it," I said showing her my hand.

"Don't you think it is bad idea for the two of us to go by ourselves?"

"My mother knows what is going on and she is going to call when they leave the station. I messaged her a picture of the address on my hand and our parents are going to meet us there later."

"My mother is going to be so mad."

"She'll get over it."

Twenty-Nine

The five hour drive to the house seemed to fly by even with the stop for gas and the bathroom break. We had made it to Edward Nilsen's house.

I pulled up behind a beige truck parked on the street a couple houses away and across the street from Sterling. The dirt on the truck was thick, as if it had been parked in the same spot and not driven for months. As I put the car in park and turned the engine off, I realized the truck may have in fact been white at one time.

"So what do we do now?" Gwen asked.

"I guess we wait. My mother should be calling soon and people will be leaving their houses to run errands for the day," I replied.

"Let me ask you something. When he brought you here, did you ever see anyone else around?" she asked.

"You know, there wasn't any one out. He didn't seem worried at all that he was going to get caught pulling someone out of the trunk of his car. I have never seen any activity here. Even when we escaped and knocked on the doors of the neighbors, no one was home," I analyzed.

"You think maybe he has taxidermied the entire neighborhood?"

"That would take years or a lot of help," I said.

"Not if he has a drug that causes suffocation," Gwen hypothesized.

"He did ask his landlord at his last known address as Sterling Bigum, how long she thought it would take to kill an entire neighborhood."

"Well, all he would have to do is break into everyone's house and inject them either while they were sleeping or over power them with a weapon."

"He would only have about four days after the victims died to finish the process," I told her.

"Why four days?" she asked.

"Well, rigor starts to set in, then all the gases inside the body build up, skin changes color, body bloats and they become no use to him," I explained.

"Maybe we should check it out," Gwen suggested.

We exited the vehicle slowly and kept low so as not to be noticed in case we were wrong. We snuck up to the house we were parked in front of. It was a small yellow house; maybe a total of two bedrooms. None of the houses in the neighborhood were built with brick. They were all wood siding and each was painted a different color than the one next to it.

We stepped onto the front porch. I crouched in front of the window and peered in. The curtain was partially open. I peeked through the opening and stood up slowly.

I fell backward and landed flat on my ass when I noticed the woman looking out the window. Her right hand was parting the curtain as though she were watching someone. When she didn't move, I stood up again. Sure enough, she was preserved, not alive, left standing in front of the window forever. She had an angry look on her face.

"He did it. He actually preserved the entire neighborhood. As soon as our parents get here we need to check out a few more houses," I told Gwen.

"Maybe it is only this street, or section of the neighborhood. It could be possible that he only murdered his immediate neighbors," Gwen spoke, unsure of what she was saying, but hopeful that there were survivors somewhere.

Just then I saw the Welsh's car pull up at a cross street and park facing the house. We crept over to the vehicle and I knocked on the driver's side window.

"Anjenette, you scared me," my mother said, rolling down the window.

"You were supposed to have called me," I scolded.

"I'm sorry, I know, but I was dealing with this one," my mother said, hitching her thumb in Doreen's direction.

"She explained the situation to me back at the station, but wouldn't tell Doreen anything until we were in the car. We spent fifteen minutes arguing over why Carrie Anne was driving our car," Laird spoke up, from the seat next to Doreen.

"What are you doing? Are you trying to put Gwendolyn in danger again?" Doreen yelled, through the open window, leaning between the front seats.

"Ya'll need to see this," I said, backing away from the car door so my mother could get out.

"See what?" Doreen asked, exiting the vehicle from the back seat. "And what are we doing here?"

"That house right there in front of you is the house your daughter and I escaped from," I explained.

"And he is the only living resident in this neighborhood," Gwen chimed in.

"How is that possible?" Laird asked.

"Just see for yourselves. Look into any window of any house and you will see," I told them.

The four of them split up and stepped up to four different houses down the street to the right of the vehicle. Gwen and I stood behind their vehicle seeming to hide in case Sterling decided to emerge from his home.

Each one of them peered into the front window of the house they had chosen. My mother jumped and let out a yelp when she noticed the person in the house. Doreen stood with her nose pressed up against the glass and expressed an "oh my goodness".

Both my father and Laird quickly descended the porches of the houses after peeping. They joined their prospective wives and led them back to where Gwen and I were waiting.

"The man in that house is most definitely dead. In no way was he preserved. He was murdered and left to rot," my father said.

"Maybe he only preserved some of the neighbors and others he left as experimentation?" I guessed.

"I don't know what happened to that boy to turn him into a psycho killer, but I think he needs some serious help," my mother said.

"What is going on here?" Doreen asked.

"I'm not sure, but we need to stop this from happening again," I replied.

"I'm calling the police to come out here right now," my mother said, retrieving her phone from the car.

My mother called Herring and informed her of the situation. Before disconnecting the call, she sighed heavily.

"What did she say?" Doreen questioned.

"She claimed they were at the local police station briefing the detectives and patrol officers about Edward Nilsen and other alias's Sterling has used. She also said if we were still here when they arrived, Jarvis would have us arrested," my mother replied.

"I'm not going anywhere. I want to make sure they arrest this bastard so I can sleep better at night knowing he is behind bars, caged like the animal he is and can't come after me again," Gwen said, crossing her arms across her chest.

"Look, why don't we just let the police do their job and relax at home with the thought that this is being taken care of," Doreen said, trying to coax Gwen into getting into the car.

"No, I want to see the arrest with my own two eyes," Gwen replied.

"Let's go for a walk. We can hang around for a little while and stay out of sight if Sterling decides to come out of the house," I told Gwen.

"Fine, but mother, you are to stay here with Dad and Carrie Anne and Wade. Do not follow us," Gwen asserted.

She turned on her heel and began walking down the street. I started a few steps behind her and power walked as fast as I could to catch up. Once I was beside her, we approached an intersection. Gwen turned to her left and walked across the street and down the next road away from our parents.

The two of us walked down one block and turned left again. We were stopped in our tracks when we saw a lady walking her dog. She was wearing a sweatshirt and jeans. We found it odd to see someone in September in Texas so covered up. Gwen and I stood there watching her.

"I don't think she is alive," Gwen said, as she took a few steps toward the woman.

"I agree. She hasn't moved or changed her expression since we spotted her," I concurred.

We realized she was preserved as well as the dog. Her expression was a frozen look of despair and the Maltese was forever to stand with her tongue hanging out, panting. We turned and started power walking back to where our parents waited.

As we approached the intersection again, we saw a light green four door sedan coming down the street the car was parked on. It was the first sign of life we had seen since our arrival.

Gwen and I hid behind a ten foot tall evergreen that was about three feet wide, in the front yard of the house on the corner. The car stopped just before the intersection. The engine cut off and a woman wearing a grey pant suit emerged from the vehicle.

Thirty

The woman was holding a clipboard and soliciting house to house. Unfortunately for her, no one answered the doors. We stayed hidden as we followed her down the street in order to get back to our parents, who were nowhere in sight.

When she went up to the door of Sterling's neighbor, we made a mad dash for my mother's car and made it without her noticing. We climbed into the vehicle, quietly closed the doors and hunkered down in our seats.

My phone rang and both Gwen and I jumped, shaking the whole car. I checked the caller ID on the screen. It was Tony. I tried to answer as cheery as I could so as not to alert him to anything.

"Hey Tony. What's going on?"

"I know you're coming home today and I just wanted to know how the conference was?" he said.

Gwen and I watched as the solicitor headed for Sterling's front door. She pressed the button to ring the doorbell and waited. Gwen leaned over me from the passenger seat. The two of us practically had our faces pressed against the driver's side window as we anticipated the opening of the door.

"Hello?" Tony said when I didn't respond.

"It was fine," I answered.

"Just fine? Did anything exciting happen?" he asked.

"I'm going to have to call you back, Tony," I told him, before ending the call.

I knew I was going to have to explain my actions to him when we got back, but at that point I didn't have time for idle chit chat.

When the wooden door finally swung open and Sterling appeared at the threshold, Gwen and I both sucked in a breath. He moved to the side and invited her into the house.

"Who's Tony?" Gwen asked, as the front door to Sterling's house closed.

"I'll tell you later. We have to save her," I said opening the driver's side door.

"What are we going to do?" Gwen asked as she climbed across the driver's seat and followed me out of the vehicle.

"Every house has a back door. We are going to get in that house," I told her.

We ran toward Sterling's house. I led the way through the side yard and quietly tried the latch on his gate to the backyard. It was locked.

"Are you sure this is a good idea?" she asked.

"Do you want to stop him and save that girl?"

"Of course, but this just doesn't seem safe," Gwen said, cautiously.

"Well then, we are going to have to climb over," I told her.

"Go ahead then. I'm not going first," she said, shaking her head.

"Okay, but you better follow me over. I'm going to need your help to take him down."

I reached up and placed my hands at the top of the fence boards. I readied to pull myself up then counted, one…two…three. I jumped as I hoisted my body up and flung one leg up and over. As I straddled the gate, I thanked God I wasn't a man. I pulled my other leg over, sat on the edge and looked down. I braced my feet against the wood, maneuvered closer to the edge and went straight to the ground below, landing on my hands and knees. Luckily the grass was soft so I only got a little dirty.

"Okay Gwenie, now it's your turn," I whispered through the fence.

She sighed heavily, then I saw her hands at the top of the fence. She did exactly what I had done, only slower and she landed on her feet. Within a couple of minutes she was standing next to me.

We pressed up against the house and moved slowly around the corner. The back door was at the other end of the house. We continued through the yard to the door.

I reached for the knob and it turned. The door popped open and I poked my head in. There was a wall to the right, a wall in front of me and a wall to the left. I saw a small opening between the wall to the left and the one in front.

We stepped in and hid in the small box just inside the door. I slid over to the opening and peeked around the corner. I realized we had entered Sterling's torture chamber. He was nowhere to be found, but there was a woman strapped to the autopsy table and she was struggling to get free.

I motioned for Gwen to follow me. We stepped up on opposite sides of the table.

"Please help me," the woman said.

I motioned for her to be quiet by placing a finger to my lips. Gwen and I began frantically unstrapping her from the table. It was the woman we saw soliciting. I was sure she was probably regretting her career choice.

The woman hopped off the table to the side where Gwen stood as my back was to the door that opened to the house.

"Anjenette, look out!" Gwen shouted.

I was grabbed from behind. Sterling had one arm around my neck and the woman took off out the door Gwen and I had entered.

"Sterling, please let her go," Gwen begged.

"No, she took you from me, yet again," he responded.

"Sterling, please. You don't want to do this," Gwen continued. His forearm pressed tightly against my trachea and I couldn't speak. He crossed the room, dragging me with him, to the tray that held his chemicals, poisons and needles and picked one up.

"If I can't have you and our baby, then neither can she," he said, as he pushed a needle into my neck and injected the entire contents into my blood stream.

"Anjenette, no! I can't live without her," Gwen screamed, tears streaking her face.

"Looks like you're going to have to now. She has just been injected with a highly lethal dose of succinylcholine. Even if the paramedics make it here in time to insert a breathing tube down her throat, she still won't make it," Sterling bragged.

I could feel the effects of the poison as my body began to go limp. Sterling opened his arm and I fell to the floor. I couldn't move and I couldn't save Gwen. I knew within minutes I would be dead.

I watched Sterling's shoes as he stepped closer to stand next to her. I fought for breath.

Within seconds the three agents and two detectives swarmed in, guns drawn and pointed at that sadistic asshole. Gwen rushed over to my paralyzed body as the agents cuffed him and recited the Miranda rights.

"Just hang in there a little longer. The paramedics are on the way," Gwen said as she stroked my hair and cried.

I gasped for air as my chest began to feel tight. I could feel my life slipping away from me. Just as I was only seeing blackness, I could feel my head being tilted back and a long plastic tube being pushed down my throat.

I could feel the manual contractions of my lungs as the EMT's pushed air into my body. I was hoisted onto a straight board and up onto a gurney. Gwen held my limp hand as I was brought out to the ambulance.

I could hear faint mumbling, but no actual words were being registered to my brain. The feeling of not having any control over my body was irritating me mentally.

I had spent two weeks in the hospital, one of which was spent completely unconscious with a tube lodged down my throat. When I had finally regained consciousness, Gwen was right there waiting for me. It was also nice to see my parents and Laird and maybe a little bit Doreen.

"Oh, Anjie. I am so sorry. If I knew he was going to do that I would never have allowed you to go into that house," Gwen said, hugging me.

"How could you have known? Sterling was unpredictable. No one could have known what he would do," I told her, after the nurse had come in and slid the endotracheal tube out of my throat. My voice was hoarse and my jaw was sore from being in the same position for so long.

"We knew he was crazy and we told ya'll not to do anything until the police arrived," Doreen scolded.

"Speaking of which, where were ya'll? When we came back around the corner none of you were near the vehicle," I said.

"We were peeping in houses to see how many he had murdered," my father said.

"We weren't peeping. We were investigating," my mother corrected.

"Oh, is that what you want to call it? Looking into someone's window is peeping," my father argued.

"Alright, so how many did you find?" I asked.

"All of them," Laird answered.

"All of them? What do you mean all of them? You mean out of the hundreds of houses in that neighborhood, he had killed everyone?" I said. I was befuddled and amazed that one man could murder an entire neighborhood.

"Well, luckily it was a retirement community so there were no children," my father said, as though he were looking on the bright side of things.

"How many of them did he taxidermy?" I asked.

"Only a few. There was one guy standing on his lawn with a water hose and even the water was fake. He was waving at the neighbor across the street who was washing his car. Not only was Sterling a psycho killer, he was also delusional. He asked the police, as they were taking him from his home, if he could at least say good bye to his neighbors," Laird informed.

"I know Sterling was arrested, but how many counts of murder is he being charged with?" I asked.

"Well, he was only charged with two hundred fifty counts of first degree murder, but five hundred counts of improper disposal of a corpse. The DA said that was enough to get him the death penalty in a maximum security prison and he is locked in a cell by himself, like the caged animal he is," Francine said, from the doorway.

"He will never murder anyone again," Tony said, peeking in from behind Francine.

"Hey, Francie. How are you? And Tony, so glad you came to see me," I said, as they approached the bed side.

"Better now that I see you are okay. Your mother called me and told me what happened, so I called Tony," Francine's tone was genuine concern.

"Now I know why you hung up on me, but why would you go back inside that house?" Tony asked.

"I could not allow him to continue his reign of terror any longer. When I saw him invite that unsuspecting victim into his house, I just knew I had to do something to help," I told them.

"I need you to stick around for a while longer," Francine said, as a single tear rolled down her cheek.

"Don't cry Francine. I'm still here. I promise I will always be here for you," I told her, gently touching her hand.

"Me too," Tony said, placing his hand on top of mine.

Thirty-One

Three months after my brush with death, Gwen decided she could no longer live in a society with all the monsters out wandering the streets disguised as humans. So, we sold the house in the suburbs and move to a secure, remote location in the country. We had purchased a four bedroom colonial style home surrounded by twenty acres of land. The house was built smack dab in the center of the property. Other than the driveway and the wrought iron gate with ten foot fencing all the way around the property, no one would know there was a house behind all the trees.

Doreen wanted to keep watch over her daughter and attempted to convince Gwen to move back in, but she maintained her independence. Unfortunately, that became the catalyst to a whole new world. Doreen decided if her daughter wouldn't live with her, then she would live with her daughter.

In one back corner of the property we had a small two bedroom cottage for Doreen and Laird, which of course, caused a domino effect of jealousy with my mother. So, a small two bedroom log cabin was built in the other back corner of the property for my parents.

The colonial had a large eat in kitchen which in turn meant we all ate together almost every night. I wasn't thrilled about living just a stone's throw away from Gwen's parents – or even my parents for that matter – but somehow we made it work.

When I quit my job at the law firm Shoney, Styles and Staff, Francine had to go with me. The partners felt as though she was too much of a liability to keep around. I started my own firm which helped victims of rape, or abusive relationships and prosecuted those who abused them. I had to do something good with my second chance at life.

I decided Francine was an asset as a personal assistant so, in order to make her life a little easier – and put a buffer between my mother and Doreen – she came to live with us. Tony thought he could be an asset to my new firm, so he joined me and we became partners. Both in business and in life. We worked out of the house, so the only one with a real commute was Tony. He stayed over some nights, but mostly still lived in his own house in order to take care of his ailing mother.

Gwen miscarried shortly into her second trimester. She was being treated for the exposure to the formaldehyde lotion. The medications she was prescribed acted almost like an abortion pill. The doctor told her it was a possibility, which in turn she was willing to risk. She wasn't comfortable knowing she was carrying the spawn of a psychopath with the possibility the baby would turn out like him.

Sterling was sitting on death row, trapped in a five by five cell for twenty three hours a day. He had requested to see Gwen twice, but each time she had turned him down. We had to request the prison intercept anymore letters he had addressed to her in order to cut off all communication. It was easier for Gwen to pretend he didn't exist if she didn't keep getting a reminder every week that he was still out there.

As for Mateo, luckily I had no idea where he was or what really happened to him. Sterling had made a reference to the fact that he had killed him, but I was sure that as soon as my guard was down he would pop up somewhere. Funny thing was, Francine felt the same way and was always on the lookout for him.

Gwen was back to never leaving the house alone and Francine was great at keeping us on schedule.

"Come on ladies. We need to go. This award isn't going to accept itself," Francine called from the living room.

A year and a half after opening Marcum and Voss, Gwen and I were getting ready to go to an awards ceremony in our honor. We were accepting an award from the Battered Women's Society for helping those in need to get out of the abusive situations they were in. We were nominated by all those we had helped. Tony and I represented the victims in their court case and Gwen helped council them into regaining their lives back. The one extra bedroom in our house was an emergency safe haven for women who need a place to stay short term.

"We're coming, hold on," I shouted from my bedroom.

I was glad to have Tony in my life, considering all the craziness that went on. Gwen was happy being single and she was glad to have Francine around due to her unusual fear of intimacy. The two of them had found the perfect mate in each other. Gwen was never alone when I went out with Tony and Francine didn't have to be affectionate with the person she wanted to spend time with. It was the perfect friendship.

I finally asked Gwen about each Monday and why she only came in on Mondays to spend the morning with me. Her answer actually surprised me.

"I only did it on Mondays because we had spent the entire weekend together and you were going to leave me for the day and I was scared. If I spent the morning with you, I could at least get in some time with you before you left for work. Once you were gone all day, I got used to it and on Tuesday I didn't need the one on one time with you because I had survived Monday alone. I knew I would be okay the rest of the week," Gwen explained.

"But every week?" I wondered.

"I can't explain my eccentricities, only my actions," she said.

"Come on Gwenie, before Francine has a total melt down for messing up her schedule. It's time to go," I said as we took one last look in the mirror at ourselves.

Gwen had her hair pinned up with curls hanging in a cascade at the crown of her head. Her floor length lavender ball gown made her look like she was going to prom, but she looked gorgeous. I chose a two piece cerulean gown. The top was lined with sequins that sparkled. The skirt was positioned on my hips and draped to the floor.

We headed out and met up with Francine who was already sitting in the car waiting.

"Finally, we are already running late," Francine said.

"Well, they can't start without us. We are the guests of honor," Gwen told her, as she smiled at me.

"In your case Gwendolyn, your mother has already called me four times to tell me that if anything happens to you, Anjenette is no longer to blame. My head will be on the chopping block," she informed, as she drove the car out of the driveway and onto the street.

"That's good to know. I wonder why I'm off the hook all of a sudden and you have become Doreen's new target," I said.

"Oh Anjenette, it's because you have Tony. My mother always said, 'Boys will make you lose your head and you won't be able to focus on anything else, especially your friends. He will replace them.' In other words my mother has insulted you without you even realizing it," Gwen said, laughing.

"So what's new with that? Your mother tends to insult me on a daily basis anyway and I just let it roll off my back," I told her, leaning back in my seat.

"Doreen has been nice to me since I moved in. She hasn't insulted me since our trip. I think we've bonded," Francine informed.

"Actually Francie, she has. Luckily, you don't interpret emotion well, so when she talks to you in a soft, slow voice, she is actually being condescending rather than nice," I enlightened her.

"That bitch. Why does she do that?" Francine wondered.

"She does that to make herself feel better." I felt bad about upsetting Francine. "Don't worry though. Usually, she doesn't feel as good doing it to you as she does to me. That is only because I notice the snarky tone in her voice. She knows that whether I say anything to her about it or not, her words really irritated me."

"Wait right here for a moment," Francine said, when we arrived to the ceremony. She got out of the vehicle and canvased the parking lot. When all was clear, she motioned for us to exit the vehicle.

We rushed into the building and joined our parents and Tony at the VIP table. Each table was set up with an elegant, almost wedding style flower arrangement in the center. My mother made it awkward as I lowered myself into the chair next to Tony and she began referencing the centerpieces as if to say Tony and I needed to get married.

Shortly after we sat down, the announcer came out on stage and stood behind the podium.

"We made it just in time," I leaned over and whispered to Gwen, who sat on the other side of me.

"Hello and welcome to the annual Battered Women's Society Humanitarian of the year award ceremony. Tonight's award is going to a couple of young ladies who have made it impossible for us not to acknowledge all the good they have done over the past year for abused women and prosecuting their abusers.

"These two have made it so much easier for abused women to come forward and face their abuser without being afraid of the repercussions or retaliation of their significant other. They have also begun construction on a new home for battered women to be able to come to and live after they have left their abusive home. There will always be a place for every abused woman to stay to help her get back on her feet.

"It is my distinct pleasure to present the Battered Women's Society Humanitarian award for the most courageous service and for the new center to be opened within the next six months. Please help me welcome, Anjenette Marcum and Gwendolyn Welsh."

The whole room erupted with applause. Gwen and I stood and made our way toward the stage.

"Why won't you just die?" a voice from behind us interrupted through the applause.

The clapping was replaced with gasps. Gwen and I turned around to see Mateo standing in the back of the room pointing a gun in our direction. He slowly moved toward us. Everyone in the room had climbed under their tables and was huddled togeth-er. Doreen, on the other hand, was trying to crawl along the floor toward Gwen, but Laird was holding her back to keep her from throwing herself in front of the gun to save her daughter.

As Mateo approached, I stood very still so as not to spook him into pulling the trigger. The barrel of the gun was aimed at my chest.

"Gwen, go over there with your parents. This doesn't concern you and there is no reason why you should be caught in the cross fire," I told Gwen, keeping my eyes locked on Mateo's gaze.

She started to move and Mateo raised the gun above his head and shot it into the ceiling. Screams infiltrated the room.

"No one is going anywhere," he said, lowering the gun so it was once again point blank at my chest.

"Mateo, what are you doing here?" I asked. The calm tone in my voice even surprised me. I was terrified.

"I am going to finish you off. One way or another, you're go-ing to die."

"I thought *you* were dead," I told him.

"Who told you I was dead? That sorry sack of shit who beat me unconscious with a tire iron? That asshole should have made sure I had stopped breathing before he walked away. Dumb ass beat me in an alley where a homeless guy saw the whole thing and used my cell phone to call the cops. I mean, sure I was in a coma for six months, rehab to learn to walk and talk again for another six, but it only took me a few weeks to get my memory back. The one thing I remember most is that I want you dead," Mateo said.

"Weren't you arrested from the convention?" I asked, touch-ing the scar on my arm.

"Without a victim, the police couldn't hold me, or charge me. If you ask me, that asshole kind of did me a favor. He got rid of you long enough for me to get released from jail, no charges pending. Then, he turned me into a victim. Win, win," he said.

"Why Mateo? Why are you so fixated on killing me?" I asked.

"I heard what you told the women in your office about me. You told them I was creepy and the mere thought of me made you sick to your stomach. And if I were to ever touch you, you would throw up. Words hurt you know," he said, raising the gun so it was aimed at my face.

"That was two years ago and in case you didn't know, you *were* creepy. Everything you ever said to any woman in the office made them all cringe with disgust, it wasn't just me," I told him.

"And yet all the others knew enough to keep their comments to themselves."

"Mateo, you broke into a woman's home and raped her. Do you really think that shouts boyfriend material? No, it does not. As a matter of fact, it screams creep. To top it all off, you broke into *my* house."

"Now you're going to pay for it," he said, positioning his finger on the trigger of the gun.

I squeezed my eyes closed so I couldn't see it coming. The gunshot made my ears ring. Everyone in the room screamed and I waited to feel the pain, or blood, or something. I slowly opened my eyes and realized I was still standing and Mateo was on the floor surrounded by a pool of blood.

I looked over at Gwen and she was standing to the right of me with a terrified look on her face, her mouth agape. I scanned the room and to my far left stood Francine with a .9 mm Beretta gripped tightly in her hands. The barrel was still smoking.

Doreen escaped Laird's grasp and ran over to Gwen. She embraced her, thankful her daughter was unharmed. Laird joined his family.

"Francine, where did you get that gun?" I asked, as everyone else emerged out from under the tables.

Francine lowered the gun, still gripping it in both hands and turned toward me. She had tears pooling in her eyes. She released the gun from her left hand as my father approached her. It was now clutched in her right hand, pointed at the floor, down by her side.

"I refuse to allow anyone else important in my life to become a victim, especially you," she said.

My mother ran over and grabbed onto me, wrapping her arms up around my shoulders. I held my gaze on Francine as I hugged my mother. My father removed the gun from Francine's hands. She was clutching it so tight he practically had to pry her fingers away from the pistol grip. Finally, her expression changed and she burst into tears. She ran over to me and wrapped her arms around me. That was the first time she had ever shown real affection toward another person.

Friendly Misfortunes is the second novel by C. L. Conolly. She has been writing since she was six years old and has studied the sadistic minds of the most infamous serial killers in order to be able to write accurately. Happily married with one child, two dogs and a cat, C. L. Conolly lives near Houston, Texas. Like her on Facebook.